Children of the Red King

Children of
the Red King

by

Madeleine Polland

Originally published by
Doubleday & Company, Inc., in 1961.

Cover art by Sean Fitzpatrick

Cover design by Ted Schluenderfritz

Hillside Education
475 Bidwell Hill Road
Lake Ariel, PA 19436
www.hillsideeducation.com

Children of the Red King

Chapter I

The soft Irish Spring came early into Connacht in the
year 1209.

It was not long since Christmas, but the grass grew green
and young on the long slope below the fort of Cormac the
Red King, and the primroses and violets already sheltered in
the rough grass about the forest edge.

A girl of nine was leaning over the tall palisade which
ringed the fort, her excited eyes fixed upon the woods. On
any other day, she would have been glad to cast her shoes
aside and run down the cool slope to pick the flowers under
the trees, but today she must remember that she was Grania,
the King of Connacht's daughter. Today the nobles of her
father's tribe would ride into the fort, ready for tomorrow's
Gathering, when they would vote upon his Heir. In times of
peace, the Gathering would have been a mighty one, with
games and dancing, and the telling of stories. All the tribal
crafts would have been on show, the copper and the beaten
gold, and the rough, warm, woollen cloth so often sought by
men from far lands overseas. But tomorrow there would be
no mighty Gathering, for any great numbers might provoke
an attack from the Normans. Only the tribe would come to

vote between her brother Fergus and her uncle Felim as to who should take her father's throne if he by any accident should die. The tribe would elect the Heir and hold the Games among themselves; governed, as always, by the ancient Law of Peace which ordered death for any man who stole or cheated or otherwise made trouble for his fellows while the Gathering was taking place.

Like the people in the village below her, Grania was dressed in her finest clothes. In the scullions' huts behind the Great Hall the servants made frantic preparation for the two days' feasting which would last far into the nights. At any moment now the first horsemen would ride from the trees and sweep up to the tall palisade where the gates stood wide open in welcome. But—and here Grania could not help laughing even as she heard her father's great voice raging in the Hall which crowned the fort—the Gathering had been called and two important people *must* be there, her uncle Felim and her brother Fergus. And now, the very day before the voting, her brother was still missing from the fort.

Almost a year before, Cormac the Red King, who wished his son to know the arts of learning as well as those of war, had sent him to the monks of the great monastery of Athenmore so that he could learn to read and write and use the fine colors and the gold with which they beautified their work. In the absence of Cormac upon another expedition the Norman advance had suddenly closed in on the monastery, and the Irish Captains had been too slow to intercept and hold back the enemy. There was no real danger to the boy as yet. The Normans at all times showed respect towards the monks and had treated the monastery with kindness, but the Abbot was afraid that they would find out that he held the King of Connacht's son, and in many secret messages he had asked for Fergus to be taken home. He was now more anxious than ever because the Normans were building a new bailey wall around the keep at Athenmore and planned to ring the abbey except for the main gate through which the pilgrims and the poor came and went. This gate, however, would be continually under Norman eyes and the task of reaching Fergus would be a thousand times more formidable.

The Irish had made a number of attempts to get the boy, but all had failed. Cormac had been wounded and could not go himself, and he roundly blamed his Captains for their useless efforts. Even as Grania listened, he was roaring his displeasure over their latest failure on the previous night.

Grania heard her name called and, looking below her to the ground, saw her foster-sister, Mairi, the daughter of Felim, her father's youngest brother. Mairi, like herself, was nine years old and as she had been Cormac's foster-child since she was very small, it had been Grania's duty to love her as a sister. She found this very difficult, for try as she might she could not love Mairi, who was thin and spiteful-looking, her hair a black cloud above her pale, narrow face. She would sting Grania with her waspish tongue, making the King's daughter betray herself with temper; and Mairi's sly blue eyes would then light up with triumph.

Now she called Grania again, saying that her father wished to speak with her.

Grania gathered up her green skirts, groping carefully down the wooden ladder from the sentry walk until her feet were safely planted on the beaten earth of the ground inside the palisade. She turned to find Mairi's blazing eyes fixed on the golden circlet that bound her hair.

"Why should you wear that?" Mairi shrilled. "The Circlet of Deirdre is for the King's wife and you are but a child as I am. How dare you wear it?"

Grania was surprised by Mairi's anger but she answered peaceably. "When my mother died, Mairi, my father swore that he would never take another wife, and it was my mother's wish that the Circlet of Deirdre should then be mine till Connacht had a wedded king once more." She touched it happily. "Today is the first time that my father has allowed me to wear it since it is so great a day."

"And you wear it to go climbing palisades! I swear it is not fair. Did I have it, I would not treat it so!"

Grania flushed in sudden fury. It was always the same with Mairi. She was continually finding Grania out in the one thing she should *not* be doing. Grania knew very well that she should not be up the palisades in her newest clothes. She should be sitting quietly in her sunny bower, built high above the palisades so that it would never lie in shadow—there she should be working with her needle, talking to her ladies and awaiting the summons of the King so that she could stand with him to bid welcome to the guests. She bit back an angry answer and Mairi went on raging, stamping her foot upon the ground.

"And why shouldn't I have the Circlet?" she cried. "Why shouldn't I have it just as much as you!"

Grania was horrified. Her anger gave way to bewilderment. What did Mairi mean? "Because, Mairi," she answered as best she could, for Mairi should know it well, "because your father is not a king and your mother did not come of Deirdre's royal line. You have no ri—"

Mairi cut her short. She stamped her foot again, and her pale eyes blazed at Grania. "Say not I have no right," she hissed. "I may have more right than you think. Wait until my father comes and see if your foolish missing brother really is the Heir. If he ever comes safe home. Wait and see."

Grania gazed frantically round. Such talk was death from a foster-child whose parents had sworn vows of faith and honor to the one who reared her. Fortunately the two girls were quite alone and while Grania still groped for words to answer Mairi, her handmaid Eithne ran out from between the huts to find her.

"Ah, there you are, my little mistress," she cried breathlessly. "I have been looking for you everywhere. Your royal father awaits you in the Hall. Come now at once."

Eithne had been nurse to the young Fergus when he was a baby, and when he grew too old to need her she had attended Grania. She knew no ceremony with the King's children and now hustled Grania urgently up the hill. "Forgive me, Eithne," the child said. "I climbed the palisade in the hope of seeing the riders coming from the woods. It should be a gay sight." She spoke absently, her eyes still fixed on Mairi, who tossed her dark head and walked away, twitching her shawl around her. "Eithne," she said slowly, "I bid you to secrecy, but I am very frightened. I do not think my Uncle Felim means well to my father. Do you think that I should tell him?"

"Tell him the prattlings of that ill-tempered child?" The plump and pretty Eithne laughed her warm, comfortable laugh. "Your father, my lady Grania, has greater things to think about than to trouble himself with that. But, mark you, he will not feel so pleased with you if you keep him waiting longer. Begone!"

Grania laughed and threw back her red hair, glad to shake off her sudden fear of evil in the tribe. Eithne is right, she thought, it is only Mairi trying to raise my temper as she always does.

She turned and ran off between the huts and up the hill slipping through the small wicket in the high defenses climbing until she reached the open space above the top palisade, in the high center of which lay the Great Hall of the King. The other huts of the King's family were grouped around it and, set apart with a guard before the door, was the House of the Holy Book, the sacred treasure of the tribe. This was a book of Gospels said to have been copied and illuminated by Columba himself before he left the shores of Ireland. In time of peace it was held before the King on all the solemn occasions of the tribe, and in time of war it went before the warriors into battle.

As Grania entered the King's Hall, she blinked in the dim light and turned her head, as always, from the forfeit hostages who sat in fetters along the walls. She could not help them, nor could she bear to see them, and even her kind father would not listen to her pleas on their behalf. "They are necessary, child," he had said, and would hear no more. Now he shouted at her from his high seat below the tribal shield. "Ha!" he said, "I thought I had lost my daughter as well as my son!"

"Your pardon, Father. I climbed the lower palisade to see the riders come. None have arrived yet."

Her father was too concerned with his own problem to think where she had been. "And is it not just as well that they have not arrived?" He banged his great fist upon the table. "For what have we to show them when they come? A tribe without an heir, a Gathering with nobody to vote on. By the Grave of Brian, I shall be the laughing stock of Ireland." He flung himself back in his chair, his long red hair falling tousled on his shoulders and his heavy eyebrows gathered in a frown across his high boned face. Red Cormac, they called him, the Red King, for his flaming hair and also for his flaming temper. He sat awkwardly, his leg pushed sideways because a wound still troubled him since his last foray against the invaders.

"Is there nothing we can do?" asked Grania quickly. Her amusement at the situation had fled before her father's anger.

"Do?" yelled Cormac. "*Yes!* My captains here would bleat about the Norman gates and beg for the boy, but that is all. But I need my son, therefore tonight I ride myself to bring him home. That is what I wished to tell you."

"But Father," gasped Grania, who knew he had not sat on a horse for many months, "your leg! You are not ready yet."

"Ready?" he roared, "Ready? What has *ready* got to do with it? I swear that I will take my leg if my leg will not take me but, by my life, my son must reach Duncormac here by dawn! Remember," he continued in a gentler voice, seeing Grania's wide and startled eyes, "I too lived in the abbey as a boy. I know it well, and know the boy's window. I will get my men to attack the other side with a noise mighty enough to draw the guards; and those who are not drawn, we shall have to kill. Then I shall need another boy, small enough to go in through the window from a horse's back and wake my son *quietly*. It must be someone that he knows, so that he will not cry out. I have been thinking through the nobles' sons—I need a brave boy who will not lose his head."

Grania's eyes had been shining more brightly as she listened and now she leaned close across the table, breathless with excitement. "Father," she said urgently, "perhaps you do not need a boy at all?"

The Red King stared at her.

"I am small and I can be brave," she went on, "and I could wake Fergus without a sound as no one else could do. When we went out at early dawn to hear the birds or to go with Dermot for the wild duck rising from the lake, I took him from his tester in the crowded Hall without a movement of the rushes on the floor. And you know that I have learned a thousand tricks on my brave mare. She would not move no matter what I did. Father, I know that I could do it, I beg you to take me."

Her father began to smile. "By all the saints, I have a brave daughter. Yes, Grania, all you say is right. I think you would do best of all. But"—he grimaced down the long Hall to where the women were grouped about the fire— "what would *they* say?"

"They need not know, Father. They need not know. I will tell only Eithne, who will get me some of Fergus's clothes. He is as tall as I, although he is younger. And after dusk, you can but say that you have found a boy to help you—Grania can lie resting in her hut."

Red Cormac leaned back and roared with laughter, the fire catching lights in the collar of fine gold about his neck. He slapped his two hands down in front of him and with difficulty heaved his heavy frame from the chair. He limped around the table and, taking Grania's face between his hands, he laughed again with pride and pleasure. "Indeed, my daughter," he said, "you are right. I have found a boy to help me. And tonight, by God's grace, he and I shall go forth to war."

Chapter II

B y dusk, all the nobles of the tribe had gathered and the camp fires of their warriors and attendants flickered through the darkening village. Round the family huts at the top of the hill were other fires for those who did not have a place within the Hall. Servants hurried about to keep them heaped with logs and turf.

A young boy slipped along the shadows in the soft dark between these fires. He was small and thin, and his woollen *lenn* hung short above his knees, but he held his shawl around him and lengthened his boyish stride as he passed close to the light. He left the fires of the nobles and the groups of talking men, and the voices, loud with ale, grew faint as he passed through the small wicket and cant quietly to the back of the stables by the lowest fence. The hill sloped up more sharply on this side of the fort and here, in addition to stables, were the huts of the scullions and of the lower servants as well as the other less important buildings of the fort. The boy could sense warm restless movement in a dark corner ahead, close against the palisade, and he caught the quiet clink of harness. The next moment he came upon a man who held three horses. As the man peered at him, his amazement changed to laughter.

"Well," he whispered, "little mistress—little master—what then do I call you for this night? Your royal father told me of your plan but I didn't think you could play the part and pass unnoticed. I own that I was wrong."

Grania smiled. "It is my hair I cannot trust, good Dermot. Eithne pinned it tightly beneath my brother's helm, but I still doubt if it will stay there. Where is my royal father?"

She took her horse and swung into the saddle as she spoke. It was a dapple grey called Macha, after the great grey steed of Cuchulain. Her eyes gleamed in the darkness. "In faith, Dermot, these clothes are better to sit a horse!"

She settled her leathers to her comfort and looked up to see the tall shape of her father limping round the corner of the stables. He, in turn, peered at Grania, breaking into a deep chuckle at what he saw. "You see, Dermot," he said, as softly as his great voice could whisper, "when necessary I have two sons but otherwise a lovely daughter. What man was better placed? Now come and help me to my horse. It is too long since I have been in the saddle."

Dermot was neither young nor very strong and it was with bursting effort that he heaved the King across his horse, the wounded leg a drag on both of them. Red Cormac sat silent for a moment in the saddle and then passed his hand across his face.

"Father," whispered Grania anxiously, "is your leg all right? It seems to me it will not take you."

He touched her hand in the darkness. "Peace, Grania," he said. "If for one night you can turn yourself into a boy to help me, can I not for the same time mend my wounded leg? Now let us go, and quickly, for there are many who would say that neither you nor I should go on this journey! I have told thirty men to await us in the forest: they will be quite enough to make a noise. I wish no fighting done tonight that we can well avoid—this is no time to catch the Norman eye. We will leave by the tall wicket to pass outside the village."

The tall wicket was the back door of the fort, guarded on the inside and invisible from without. Dermot whispered to the sentry who hastily unbarred the door, glancing curiously at the boy who rode beside his king. They passed through in single file, her tall father bending in the saddle, and then they were on the steep green slope that led down into the forest.

"Hurry now," said Cormac, "or else the moon will rise before our work is done. Let Dermot lead and follow him closely. I will attend you at the rear."

Dermot wheeled his horse and Grania followed. In a few moments they had gained the shelter of the forest where the darkness closed round them and only the sure feet of their horses guided them until they came to the wide path that led to Athenmore. Grania turned her head at a noise behind her—the thirty men were following, having joined them in silence from the darkness of the trees. Grania shivered. She was not afraid nor had she felt afraid at any moment for she was wrought up to such excitement with the cool wind upon her face, her strong and gallant Macha held between her knees and the beating hooves behind her, that she gave no thought to Normans or to danger.

They rode in this way for the two hard hours it took them to reach the townland's edge of Athenmore; and where the forest bordered on the green fields the Red King called his men to halt and spoke to them.

"You have your orders from your captain. I need but to remind you. You will go to the main drawbridge of the keep— it is not working yet and gives them no safety. Come up to it from the shadow of the woods with a great noise and shouting and blowing of your horns as though you would attempt to cross. Should they attack, retreat at once into the woods. I do not wish you to fight but to keep them occupied. Should they return into the keep, then come once more and draw them out. When your captain hears the three long notes of Dermot's horn, he will know that we have finished our task and you must make all haste to meet us here. Now go, and God be with you in your work."

At a word of command from the captain, the troop turned and cantered quietly away along the soft grass under the trees.

Grania turned to her father, who was shifting restlessly in his saddle, easing and stretching his wounded leg. In the grey light that came before the rising moon, his face looked ghastly to the anxious child.

"Father," she said, "is it not too much? Can't I and Dermot go now and get my brother and bring him to you here?"

The Red King smiled. "You are indeed a brave young son tonight and I thank you. But no. My leg and I will fight well enough if need be. Now we must go forward."

The meadows stretched long and flat from the side of the castle where the Abbey lay, so there was no secret way to reach the gates. They had to ride as quietly as they could across the level grass, fording the river below the monastery's very walls where the great new church now reared its bulk against the lightening sky. They stood in the shadow of the wall, their horses fetlock-deep in water, waiting for the sounds that would tell them they could move.

"Dermot," ordered the Red King, "give me your horse and spy beyond the corner of the wall to see what sentries stand before the abbey gate."

Dermot handed over his reins and then slid gently and with the greatest caution down into the water, creeping along the dark wall of the church until he could look round it to the open ground between the river and the gates. Equally slowly he crept back.

"Sir," he whispered, "there is not much light to see, but to my eyes there is only one moving sentry. There are, however, two tents in front of the gate in which there may be more."

"Enough," said the King, and at that moment the noise of a fierce battle broke out from the distance, followed by the flare of winding horns from the shadowy keep. They edged the horses to the corner of the church, easing them up out of the river and now they saw four soldiers running from the tents and round the abbey wall in the direction of the keep. The sentry stayed before the gates.

"He is yours, Dermot," breathed Red Cormac. "Now Grania, do exactly what I bade you when we talked."

They drove their spurs into their horses and turned them to the abbey; Dermot first, with his sword bared for the startled sentry, who died without a sound. Once inside the gates they went more gently, sidling their excited horse across the wide court and round one wing of the sprawling wooden buildings that made up the monastery.

"Quiet now, Macha, quiet," Grania whispered, fondling the neck of the uneasy grey and thinking it was as well her father knew his way, for here, in the thick darkness, she could see nothing but the black walls that loomed about her.

Then her father stopped and the restless movements the horses and the faint clink of their harness seemed to fill the night with noise. "Now Grania," he said, "this is the sleeping-room for all the boys. Find your brother with speed for the noise beyond the keep has stopped and I not know what that may mean."

"Come, gently now, Macha," she coaxed into her horse's ear. "Come up, now." She edged her up below the dark shape of the window which her father had shown her; then she spoke to her again. "Now, stand Macha. Stand till I return."

Giving her reins to her father, she stood upon the horse's back. The window was a little way above and covered by leather blind. It would not be easy. She put her hands upon the sill and pulled herself upwards, scrabbling vainly for a foothold in the wooden wall.

"QUIET," hissed her father and the grey stirred restlessly.

Then her feet held a rough place in the wood, leaving her one hand free to push aside the leather curtain and she was able to pull herself into the room. It was long and narrow and very, very dark but at the far end a tiny wick floated its little light before a shrine and, thankfully, Grania groped her way to this. Picking up the lamp, she crept along the beds that lay against the wall, peering at each in the faint light and breathing out a prayer of gratitude as, at the fourth bed, she saw her brother's head upon the skins.

"Fergus," she whispered softly and clearly, kneeling beside him on the floor. "Fergus, wake! It is your sister—Grania. Wake! Fergus!"

Fergus woke instantly, without moving, his eyes bright and wide in the light of the little lamp. Even in this desperate moment, Grania smiled and thought, "I told my father it was always like this with him." Then she laid her hand upon his shoulder. "Listen, Fergus, do not move until I tell you what to do. Beneath the window at the end there stands my horse. Drop upon her back as quickly and as quietly as you can and I will follow you. Our father waits beside her."

The boy got up without speaking. He crept towards the un-covered window, followed by his sister, who first took time to put the little lamp safely back on the shrine. When they were halfway down the room, one of the sleeping children cried aloud and sat up in his bed. Grania gasped and turned as if to silence him, but Fergus held her arm.

"He is the deepest sleeper of us all," he whispered. "He sees nothing."

Grania looked doubtfully at the child once more and went on after her brother. In a few moments he was out of the window and had dropped onto the sturdy back of Macha.

"Come up behind me, son, and let your sister follow," whispered the Red King. "She has done well to get you."

Fergus slipped across onto his father's horse and clasped his arms round his waist. Only then did he really understand that this was no dream, and he pressed his face into the rough wool of Cormac's cloak, hiding the hot tears that shamed him.

As Grania dropped easily onto Macha's back she noticed with half her mind that the noise beyond the keep had started once again. By now the moon was rising and the courtyard was flooded with a pale revealing light.

"All speed, now!" her father cried, and lashed in with his spurs, leading them at a gallop across the court and out of the abbey gates. As they splashed through the river in a whirl of silvered water, they heard shouts behind them and the trembling whine of an arrow, and then another, passing by their heads. But they bent over their horses and rode headlong for the forest. Dermot alone lifted his face and let the long notes of his horn ring out three times across the moon-bleached fields.

Safe within the shelter of the forest the Red King drew rein. "Well, Dermot," he said, when they had gained their breath, "what do you think of the boy I got to help me? Did he not do well? Grania, this has been a good night's work—it took you

17

and me to get the boy. How is he getting on behind me?" He clasped the child's hands against his waist. "I am longing to look at him but this is no time. We must be ready to ride at once as soon as our men come back. Isn't that wise, my soldier daughter?"

A clear, familiar, merry laugh rang out in the quiet night from the small figure behind the King. "Indeed, my Father, you do well to say your soldier daughter, for no one now could think to say she was your soldier son. Oh, sister, your hair has hopelessly betrayed you!"

As her father's deep laugh rumbled below the child's treble, Grania put up her hand and felt her hair. One long lock fell rippling down her back from beneath the padded helm. She pushed at it hopelessly and her father bade her leave it.

"I hear the troop," he said, "and we must haste for home. Your hair is of no matter now. The women will forgive me anything for saving the Heir. Well, Rory," he said to the captain who rode up beside them, "how did the noise go?"

"I swear, Sir, it was most successful. I think the Normans are still puzzling as to what really happened."

"And they will puzzle more," said Red Cormac. "For when the morning comes and the old Abbot finds that one small bed lies empty, he will do no more than say his *Deo Gratias* and leave the Normans with their questions. Now, we gallop for Duncormac." And he spurred his horse to lead the cavalcade towards home.

The broad ride through the woods lay clear and pallid, stretching away before them in the moonlight, and they rode fast with their heads down for they were by now within their own country and should have nothing to be afraid of. Grania had fallen a little way behind her father as they rode, so that when the arrow whistled from the forest on her left, missing

the boy behind the king, it hissed so closely past her head
that she felt its hot breath on her skin.

"Attend it, Dermot," roared the King. "I will take the
children."

Almost without pause Dermot wheeled the troop into the
woods, crashing through the small growth beneath the trees
while Cormac and his son and daughter galloped for the shelter
of the fort. This time they did not seek the secrecy of the wicket
but thundered up the long slope from the trees to where the
gates stood open in the palisade in order that everyone could
freely come and go on this nigh of celebration. They did not
draw rein until they reached the Hall and, by that time, the
word had spread like summer-fire that the King had brought
his son. More wood was thrown upon the dying fires and the
feasting and the merrymaking began again to celebrate the
good news, filling the long hours till daylight.

Meanwhile, the King sat with his children in the quiet
candlelight of Grania's bower, his leg upon a stool and his
face heavy with the thought of what the random arrow might
portend. Could the Normans be massing in the forest to attack
the gathered tribe? Or was it one wandering soldier, hoping
for advancement by a lucky shot?

Eithne clucked about the children like a mother hen, calling
for warm drinks as she wrapped a cloak around the half-dressed
boy and lifted the heavy helm from Grania's tired head. As
she did this, her cheerful face puckered and she gave a loud
cry of dismay."

"Your hair, my little mistress, your lovely hair! What harm
is this?"

When Eithne had released it from the pins beneath the
helm, Grania's long red hair had tumbled down below the
stool on which she sat. All except the lock that had fallen as

she galloped from the abbey, the lock that Fergus and her father had laughed at in the woods. The arrow from the trees had sheared it off her head, leaving a ragged gap in the bright gold.

Even as Eithne fussed and grieved and the Red King reproached himself for having led her to such danger, Dermot asked permission to come up and entered with an arrow in his hand.

"We found no one, sir," he said, "but this we found embedded in the tree where you had passed. Look!"

Dermot handed him the arrow and the King gazed at it in silence for a long time. Then he threw it on the table.

"I would prefer," he said heavily, "it were the greatest Norman army that I have ever faced." He bent his red head upon his hand.

Grania looked over at the arrow. In the smoky light of the candle that stood beside it on the table she could see quite clearly why her father grieved. It was an Irish arrow.

Chapter III

A nd so when the morning of the Gathering dawned blue and fair, the King's son slept safely in his own bed of carved yew, set beside that of his father in the King's Hall.

The usual place for the assemblies of the tribe was in a vast clearing in the forest but it was very close to Athenmore and thought to be too dangerous. For this reason, the wicker hurdles marking the enclosures, one for the men and one for the women, had been placed below the village, and the sports that followed on the voting would be held on the open ground that lay between the enclosures and the woods.

Grania came early to sit in her place on the wooden platform for the noble ladies which stood at the front of the women's enclosure. Today she walked formally, closely attended by Eithne and followed by Mairi and the other ladies of high rank who were her company. The folds of her skirt were made of yellow silk bought from the foreign traders at some earlier Gathering; as she walked, a rich embroidery glowed and shimmered round the hem and where her tunic opened at the breast. Her gold fringed shawl was fastened on her shoulder by the Brooch of the High King and the precious Circlet of Deirdre lay round her burnished hair. On such occasions it was her duty as the King's daughter to have reached her place before her father came to take his throne, but it was a duty which pleased her for she loved to be able to watch him as he came.

First of all, the Holy Book, boxed in gold, was carried before him by a young warrior. Next came the man who held her father's shield and after that his sword-bearer. This was no sword of ceremony but his own huge two-bladed sword sheathed in copper and laid in gold with which he had done much to carve the history of his tribe. Then came her father himself. He looked magnificent, a head taller than any of the nobles and surrounded closely, as always, by his bodyguard of four freed men. Today, Grania noticed that he only limped a little and the heavy folds of his superb embroidered *lenn* concealed the binding on his leg. The vivid patterns of the embroidery shot with gold gleamed across his mighty chest, and a sheen of misted light lay round him, struck from the heavy bracelets on his wrists, the Brooch of Tara that held his shawl upon his shoulder, and the complex whorls of the royal diadem over his brow.

Behind him walked his son, fair and slender in comparison with his father but with a strong young dignity and very royal in his gleaming clothes and ornaments of ceremony.

Next in the procession came the lesser kings and chiefs of the clans that made up the tribe—a blaze of brilliant clothes and precious metals. Her uncle Felim walked foremost among them, the only other candidate that would be judged today for the succession. As he passed, Grania looked at his small unfriendly eyes that seemed to be watching the occasion but not taking part in it, and she felt the same uneasy fear that she had known before when her foster-sister had made her angry hints and again when her father had held the Irish arrow in his troubled hands.

The chief judge of the tribe sat high upon a stone seat above the crowd where he had an extensive view over the whole Gathering. It was he who would count the voting for the Heir and give the final judgement in the contests. When the King was settled in his huge chair and all the nobles round him, the judge gave the sign that he was ready to begin and that the Bard of Cormac should step forward to read the pedigree of Fergus.

Grania had never known a time when old Caffa had not been her father's bard, and the sound of his voice in accompaniment with the harp was one of her strongest childhood memories. Now she watched with affection as the bent old man came slowly forward, his long grey bardic robes, pale against the vivid colors of the crowd, sweeping the young grass. He had no need to read the pedigree of Fergus even if he could, for he knew it all by heart just as he had known it years ago when he was young and had his sight and the boy, Cormac, was chosen as Heir to his father Murdoch Morann. Caffa had scorned to read the pedigree then, just as he scorned to have a young man read it for him now. When, leaning upon his staff, he had been guided to his place beneath the judge's chair, he turned towards the crowd. Slowly, in his fine old voice and with a calm certainty, he began to recount the long line of the generations, going back through the centuries to the earlier Fergus and dwelling on the old names of Ireland with reverence and pride.

There was silence all the time he spoke and when he stopped a long, deep sigh escaped the crowd. They shuffled their feet restlessly and stared with curiosity as the Bard of Felim took the old man's place. He was tall and proud and used every art of voice and gesture to enhance the story that he read from off a parchment in his hand. But all his gestures and the richness of his strong voice could not conceal the fact that Felim's pedigree was shorter and, in places, left the true blood.

When he had finished, the judge called the candidates to stand and Fergus and Felim advanced side by side upon the royal platform. Grania felt Mairi stir in her chair behind her and silently prayed for her small, fair brother, who looked so frail and young beside the toughened warrior at his side. It was possible that, in such troubled times, the tribe would feel it safer to place the succession in the hands of Felim rather than in those of a child, even though he was the King's son. While she looked at them, the judge had been speaking to the nobles, telling them that now they had heard the pedigrees, it was their place to vote. He asked those who wished for Felim Dhu Morann to show their hands first.

From his high seat, he counted fifteen votes and Grania knew by the colors of their *lenna* that they were all from Felim's tribe. Felim's face went black and he made as if to turn and go, but, catching his brother's eye, he remained to watch the mighty show of hands for Fergus, undoubted Heir of the Morann tribe. The Red King got up and went to stand beside his son, and, with his father's hand upon his shoulder, Fergus faced the noisy acclamations of his tribe. Grania was filled with love and pride as she watched them and was only sorry that the strict conventions of the Gathering forbade her to rush across and congratulate her brother.

With the business of the day now safely over, the tribe could turn to pleasure, and soon contests were taking place in the green arena. This was the first big *Feis* that Grania re-membered and she found so much to watch that it was hard to know where to look. Along one edge of the field the athletes were running races, some on level ground and some over the wicker hurdles that were placed across the course. From the middle of the grass there frequently came the dull thump of a heavy stone, followed by the pacer measuring the length it had been thrown. The men that cast the stone were the heaviest of the tribe, and Grania knew her father had always led the sport in this and many other games. She felt he must be sad today to be so thwarted by his leg and she turned to look and perhaps to smile at him. The royal throne was empty. Only Fergus was standing by the vacant chairs talking excitedly to some young boys of his own age who stood below. It did not take her long to find her father for she knew where he would be. Down at the edge of the field where the hurdles laid the course around the hill, the horse racing was about to start and Cormac was there to whisper instructions to his rider.

Grania smiled and turned to speak her thoughts to Mairi, who looked away, however, and pretended not to hear, a flush of anger on her face and bright tears in her eyes.

"Mairi," she said kindly, laying her hand upon her arm, "do not be so disappointed. You must have known that they would choose my brother. There was no real reason why they should not."

Mairi shook off her hand without a word and turned her back despite the shocked glances of the women round about. Grania shrugged and turned back to the games.

Throughout the long day the sports went on, the wrestling and the jumping and the throwing of spears, while in the quiet corners of the field the story-tellers of the tribe were surrounded by eager listeners. The greatest crowd was round the story-teller of the King who, by repute, had to know stories up to seventy times seven so that his listeners would never tire. Through the warm noon hours, the servants came and went with ale and simple food to sustain the company until the feast of the evening and, as the day wore on, the competitions moved towards their ends. One by one, the men who were defeated left the games and the winners moved on to meet each other until a champion was found in every sport.

In the late golden afternoon, as the sun moved low around the hill, the crowd had gathered to watch the wrestling. As might happen at any Gathering, the last bout was between the King's brother and a strange young warrior, a follower of another chief who had been bidden to the fort. Felim was the older and with his ceremonial clothes thrown aside, he looked thin and slight beside the tall young soldier whose muscles ran like living things beneath his freckled skin. But the Red King knew that Felim's slenderness was that of strength and in his great voice roared encouragement to his brother.

In the long contest before the frenzy of the shouting crowd, Cormac was proved right. At the final crushing lock the shoulders of the young warrior were forced to the ground by painful inches and Felim stood erect with a smile of satisfaction on his face. He took great pride in his strength and rejoiced to be the victor, feeling safe today from challenge from the King, who was his only equal.

Then, suddenly, Grania saw her father begin to take off his shawl and lay aside his diadem. The nobles crowded round him to protest while Felim's face had lost its smile and wore an angry look of disbelief.

"Surely my father cannot be going to wrestle," Grania cried. "His leg is not yet fit and he will come to harm."

But her father *was* about to wrestle. To the curdling yells of his excited tribe, who encouraged every exploit of their brave, flamboyant leader, the Red King stepped down to face his brother. He was laughing and in a high good humor.

"Come, Felim," he cried, "let us try our strength against our handicaps. You are tired with many bouts, and I have only one leg so I think we should stand equal. Are you ready?"

He did not seem to see that Felim foamed with sullen rage. Could his elder brother not leave him with one small victory without challenging it? This was no sport to Felim, and he moved in to start the bout with his face so dark with fury that Grania clapped her hands over her eyes and could not look.

"Are you afraid your precious father will be hurt, for he might well be." Mairi's voice hissed quietly behind her.

Grania did not answer. She forced herself to lower her hands and look calmly at the wrestling men and the tribe flocking to the hurdles to roar encouragement at their King. He needed it, for the wounded leg seemed too great a handicap, and time and again the crowd fell breathless as the huge shoulders were inched towards the ground by Felim, who wrestled with fury as well as with skill. Gradually the tribe grew quiet for they sensed that there was more in this than mere sport and they felt abashed by Felim's onslaught on their King within the rules of peace that bound the Gathering. They longed for Cormac to win but, like Grania, could hardly bear to look for fear that he might not.

For a long time it seemed that Cormac battled for his life and then, when all the silent crowd could do was to wait for the end, the figures on the slippery grass seemed to convulse and leap apart. When they joined again for the necessary seconds, the shoulders of Felim were on the ground.

The Red King got up. He was still smiling before the frenzied excitement of his people, but barely standing on his wounded leg. He gave his hand to Felim, who ignored it and would have gone away without a word. Grania saw her father cease to smile and noticed his sharp command to Felim, who halted stiffly and with bad grace walked back onto the royal platform beside his brother. Grania, however, had seen her uncle's face in that unguarded moment as he got up from the ground and all her fears returned a hundredfold. Her father had forbidden that the arrow should be mentioned that day, but he did not seem to see the danger that lay in front of his eyes or think from how near home the arrow might have come. There was nothing that she could do, and she sighed and turned away.

"Come, my ladies, we must make ready for the evening."

Once again Mairi looked aside and would not meet her eyes.

The ladies of the fort did not attend the feast but went to the Hall, when it was over, to listen to the singing of the bards and the old legends of the story-tellers. Grania sat in her bower to wait. From its high windows she could look down on the crowded scenes of celebration in the space below. The nobles who had no seat in the Hall had gathered round the fires and the flames glowed on their colored clothes and winked in their gold and silver ornaments; the servants rushed about between the fires with ale and food Talk ran high about the doings of the day, and shouts and laughter chased the tumblers and the jesters as they gamboled through the crowd. The smoke hung gently in the soft windless evening, and the steep roof of the King's Hall climbed black against a green, translucent sky, outlined above the doors and windows from which the light streamed out across the revelers.

The Hall was as crowded as the space outside when Grania came to take her place beside her father later in the evening. The smoke was drifting thick below the great beams of the roof, dimming the colors of the shields that hung above the chairs. The nobles at the long, carved wooden tables faced the huge fire burning in the middle of the floor and from its four corners tall candles threw a lurid smoky light that flashed a million times in the gold and silver and the beaten bronze of ornaments and tableware.

Grania sat beside her father's chair throughout the long evening as the story-tellers came in turn to take their place beside the fire, telling the oft-repeated, but well-loved stories of the golden days of Ireland and her illustrious kings and saints.

They told the story of Cuchulain, the Hound of Ulster, who, although he had been the enemy of Connacht, was known as Ireland's greatest warrior. Then they spoke of Columba, who, together with his band of monks, had left Ireland for Iona and had built a monastery there from the rough stones of the island. The story of Patrick followed, another saintly man who brought the word of God to Ireland itself, and of the fierce Brian whose beautiful palace at Kincora was a meeting-place for the whole world.

After many stories had been told, the bard of the King himself came to the fire. His tale was the tragedy of Deirdre who had been brought up in solitude by Connor, King of Ulster, so that she might be his bride. But she saw and fell in love with Naoise, one of the three sons of Usna, and escaped with them to Scotland, where he and his two brothers built her a sunny bower in the apple grove on Loch Etive. There they could pull the salmon from the river at the door and take the wild deer off the hill with an arrow from the window. She lived in perfect happiness with Ainle and Arden and Naoise, the most handsome of them all. Then, in his vengeance, King Connor had slain the three sons of Usna and, mad with grief, Deirdre had thrown herself into their open grave to die.

As the story-teller's voice grew soft and died, Cormac reached forward for a harp and moved towards the fire. He sat for a moment in the firelight, his fine hands plucking gently at the strings and his eyes dreaming on the glowing flames. Then he plucked the harp more strongly and began to sing. It was the ancient *Lament for Deirdre* that he sang, so sweetly and so sadly that Grania marveled, as always, that this was her father of the roaring warrior's voice. She looked round the vast, smoke-shadowed hall in which all the lesser kings and chiefs and nobles of her tribe were gathered, and listened to her father's voice lamenting the dead queen whose circlet she wore on her hair. A warmth of pride rose up within her. This was her tribe, and her father was the King; her brother was the Heir, and this was her much-loved home. No one, she felt suddenly, had a more perfect life than she did. In her rush of happiness she lifted up her hands and laid them on the Circlet in her hair, touching it with love and satisfaction.

At that moment, she felt a glance upon her and, turning round, she met such a blaze of hate from Mairi's eyes, that all her happiness was banished and she was left trembling and unheeding through the last soft notes of Cormac's song.

Chapter IV

It was late before Grania retired into her own hut to be wrapped by Eithne in her warm sleeping-robe and to creep gratefully between the soft skins of her carved bed.

"Oh, Eithne," she said wearily, "I am so tired. It has been a wonderful day. Didn't you think my father and my brother looked very noble?"

"You truly looked your father's child yourself, my little lady. But, yes, your brother did look well." She sighed and her comfortable face grew wistful in the candlelight. "It is a great position for a lad so young as seven. It seems only yesterday that he lay in my arms, and now he stands Heir to all the State of Connacht."

Grania laughed at her. "You would much prefer him still to be a baby. Come, Eithne, we must all grow up."

"Indeed, yes," Eithne smiled back. "I would hold Fergus to my skirts too long. He is his father's son and so must take his place. Now, sleep, Lady Grania, for it is very late."

"Tell me, Eithne, did you put my Circlet safely away? It is my greatest treasure."

"I did, indeed I did. I have laid it in the chest, where it belongs. Now I beg you sleep and God be with you for the night."

"God keep you safe, Eithne."

Grania snuggled beneath her skins. She heard Eithne settle in her own bed across the room, and it was not long before her even, gentle breathing told Grania that she was asleep. But, tired and sleepy though she was, Grania could not follow her. She lay and watched with drowsy eyes the candle flickering on the domed ceiling of her bower. Her father, who so loved beauty and wished to teach his children to love it too, had ordered all the inside of her room to be smoothly plastered over and then painted white. Then he had got the finest artists of the tribe to paint the walls and ceiling with colored woodland flowers. As she lay, it seemed as if the flowers and ferns and little leaves were moving in the flickering light, as though, she thought, a wind had whispered through a forest glade in summer. She smiled with sleepy pleasure, but the thought of the forest reminded her of the arrow. She felt sure she knew to whom it belonged, but while they all lay under the Peace that bound the Gathering, an accusation of her uncle was too terrible to think of. Her father would never hear a word against his brother, whose evil tempers he humored as the whims of a petted younger boy.

"But my uncle Felim is no longer young," thought Grania wisely, "and I am sure he means to harm my father."

Her weary mind whirled round and round upon her trouble. She thought of Felim's face when the King beat him at the wrestling. Why could her father not see? She thought, too, of the look that Mairi had given her as her father was singing the old lament. What did Mairi and her uncle Felim want? Wasn't it enough that she had to worry about the Normans for her father without having to fear what his brother might do to him?

Grania would have said that she had not slept at all when she spoke about it afterwards, but it was against the pale light before the dawn that she saw the curtain of her door lift up as somebody went out. She just had time to notice that the shape was small and to see a breath of wind lift a cloud of hair before the curtain dropped again,

"Eithne!" she called frantically. "Eithne!" She jumped from her bed and snatched at her cloak. "Eithne, wake up! Somebody was in the room, and I am sure it was Mairi."

Eithne roused herself more slowly. "Peace, little mistress, peace. We will light a fresh candle and then we shall see. And if Mairi was in your room, well then indeed, why not? Perhaps she wanted me and then did not like to wake me. There! Here is a new light, and look, the room is just as it was last night; nothing has been touched and no one harmed. Perhaps you had a dream."

"No, Eithne, no. It was Mairi. I saw her hair quite clearly against the light before the curtain fell back. You know that she is the only person who has that soft clouded hair, and I know she means harm."

Grania shivered as she spoke, and anxious tears rose to her eyes. How could she tell Eithne of her terror of her uncle Felim and his child? She felt their threat about her like a cloud, but no one would believe her and, under the Law of Peace, she could not even speak. She turned hopelessly to Eithne, who gathered the shaking child into her arms.

"Peace," she said again. "Peace, little Lady Grania. Mairi is only a young girl like yourself. How could she harm you or your father? And your uncle Felim is your father's youngest brother, only chief of a minor state. If the Red King must fear *him* then we have reached a sorry plight. You are exhausted riding through the long night before the Gathering, and your mind is full of phantoms. I will go to a fire and make you a warm drink so that you can sleep again till day. And do not speak these things abroad, for remember the Peace is binding, even on the King's daughter."

Grania allowed herself to be coaxed back to bed, where she lay and waited for Eithne to return. Even if she could speak, how could she put her terror for her father into words? She must be patient and keep quiet. If all went well, her uncle would be gone by sundown and surely Mairi by herself could do no harm. When Eithne came with the warm soothing drink, Grania took it quietly and, helped by the herbs, was soon peacefully asleep. When she woke again, the noises of the busy life within the fort sounded loud below her and brilliant sunshine was pouring through the windows of her bower. It showed her Eithne, standing at the curtains of her bed. Her cheerful rosy face was pale and stricken, and her mouth worked without producing words. Grania sat bolt upright, filled with fear.

"What *is* it, Eithne? What *is* it. Tell me!"

"My Lady Grania," she burst out. "You were right. If only I had given chase last night instead of hushing you, we might have saved this dreadful thing." She began to weep in anguished gasps. "Now your father will blame me, and a crime within the middle of the Peace means death. Oh, God have mercy!"

"Eithne!" Grania jumped out of bed and seized Eithne by the arms. "Eithne, I beg you, tell me what it is."

"The Circlet of Deirdre is stolen from the chest. That is the reason Mairi came last night. And all I did was bid you hush and let her go."

Grania dropped her hands and stared at Eithne for a moment and then walked slowly over to the chest of carved and gilded yew that stood beyond her bed. All her ornaments, her torques of twisted gold, the fine worked crescents that she wore round her neck, her bracelet girdles and the fillets that she used to bind her hair, all were there. The great gold brooches that she used to hold her shawls, even the glorious copy of the Royal Brooch of Tara that the High King had given her, all these were there. But in the padded satin tray that had been shaped to hold the Circlet, there was nothing.

"I went to get out your crescent collar, and there I found the Circlet missing. At the Gathering of the Heir, for his relatives to rob the King! This is the most dreadful thing that I have ever known." Eithne was distraught and great tears rolled down her cheeks.

"Hush, Eithne, hush, I beg you! This will do no good. Oh, peace, peace, I cannot think. Help me put on clothes. We must go to my father at once."

Grania herself was appalled. The Law of Peace was so strict that she knew it was most unusual for even the smallest quarrel to arise, and now the King's own property was stolen by somebody attending the election of his son. Grania was too shocked to cry, and she fumbled desperately to get on all her clothes so that she could go quickly to put her troubles to her father.

"Come, Eithne, now, I don't want you to weep anymore. Tidy yourself to go before my royal father. He will know exactly what to do."

Eithne washed her face and straightened out her gown before following her small mistress across to the King's Hall. Grania acknowledged the greetings of the nobles absent-mindedly; they were hurrying to leave, for, in the present dangerous times, no one wished to be away from home too long. As she came up the Hall, she was dismayed to find her uncle Felim sitting by her father, and Mairi standing at his side.

As Grania stood hesitant, uncertain what to do, Mairi stared at her, with malice in her light eyes. Grania could not speak in front of her uncle and her cousin. Then her father spoke first.

"Ah, daughter," he said, "you come to hear sad news. Your uncle Felim has decided to take Mairi home for a while to visit with him. But she will return in time to Duncormac."

"She will indeed," said Felim, and Grania glanced at him, feeling that his words were not as pleasing as they were meant to sound. He, like his daughter, was dark and pale, and Grania had always disliked the mean expression of his thin-lipped mouth. Even as a small child, she had run away from his caresses, and now she felt the falseness of the smile he turned upon her father. But the Red King would never see any wrong in Uncle Felim, and if Grania mentioned her dislike of Mairi, her father always dismissed her, and told her not to be jealous.

Now Cormac drew Mairi close to him, and Grania stiffened to see her cousin place her arm round her father's neck.

"We shall miss her, shall we not, Grania? She has been your sister through these years, but now I am afraid we must allow her father to have her for a time."

Mairi's eyes regarded Grania steadily as she stood within the King's arm, waiting for the polite agreement that was Grania's duty. But at that moment Grania was unable to behave as duty required.

"Father," she said desperately, "I beg forgiveness of my Uncle Felim and my Cousin Mairi, but I must speak with you alone."

Cormac's thick red eyebrows shot up his forehead and he looked at Grania coldly. "I trust your words shall be sufficiently important to merit such a discourtesy."

"Do not be angry with me, Father." Grania was on the verge of tears. "I would not ask you if it were possible to do otherwise."

"Can you not speak in front of your uncle? Or can it not wait?"

"No, my Father, NO!"

Grania saw Mairi's eyes slide to catch her father's. They exchanged a brief glance and then Felim stood up.

"Well, I will not hold the child, Brother," he said easily. "Let her speak to you, and I will go and oversee the servants load my horses, for we must ride before the sun is high. It is no doubt some childish prattle of a broken toy."

Grania moved sharply to avoid the hand he would have laid upon her head, and then, bidding Eithne to follow them to the door to see that they had safely gone, she waited in silence until they had left the Hall.

Her father was working up his anger. "What mummery is this?" he shouted. "You cast my brother from the Hall and post your servant to see that he has gone. I think, Grania, that you forget yourself, for all you are my daughter."

"Dear Father, curb your rage and do but listen," begged Grania; and then she told him her story, beginning at the morning of the day before, when Mairi had screamed her jealous rage about the Circlet and her vague threats against Fergus.

"The arrow!" said the Red King suddenly.

"Yes, Father, I thought so all along."

Her father sat quiet for a few moments; then, easing his leg carefully from the stool that held it, he stood up.

"I ask your pardon, Grania." He laid his hand on her shoulder. "I shout too easily before I listen."

"But, Father, what can you do?"

"Indeed, what can I do?" her father answered. "I cannot deny that your cousin Mairi has so forgotten the bonds of fosterage that she has robbed my house—and within the Peace. But that my brother Felim threatens me, my person or my

throne, that, Grania, is too deep a wound for me to take at
once. As yet, we cannot be sure. And, as to Mairi, what can
we prove? Your foolish girl here let her go." Grania heard
Eithne gulp behind her. "So," her father continued, "if she has
hidden the Circlet well and I order a search only because I am
suspicious and find nothing—well, I and not my brother or his
child have broken the Peace and my death might be their easy
satisfaction. I am afraid that our hands are bound unless we
find out something more before they leave. Do not grieve for
your jewel, child. If we have lost it, then we have lost other
things of greater value as well. Go now and leave me to think
about this. Behave just as you normally do and do not tell
anyone what you know. And, on your way round, send me
your brother. And bid that girl stop sniveling," he bellowed
in a sudden rage.

Eithne, who had now almost ceased to breathe, stood aside
as Grania, after pausing to look back at her father, passed out
through the door. He stood with his hand upon the huge King's
candle that always burned in front of his chair. Its smoky light
fell on his red head that was sunk between his shoulders, and
his eyes were on the floor.

"I wish he would rage and shout as he usually does," said
Grania, "I cannot bear to see him so stricken. There is my
brother, Eithne. Ask him to go to my father."

Grania turned towards the wooden stairs that led up to
her bower. She knew that she should wish God's speed to the
departing guests but, for the moment, she was tired of being
a king's daughter. She wanted to get up where she could see
the mountains and the blue hills. She leaned upon her outside
window and looked down across the teeming fort, and beyond
the pasture lands, to where the small fields lay tawny in the
sunlight, crossed and recrossed by the narrow walls. Today

her hills were brown and green as gold, turning to cool blue and warmed again to color as the clouds sailed away from the sun. Grania laid her head against the window, and the hills grew misty through her tears.

"Do not grieve for your jewel," her father had said. But how could she not, for she loved it more than anything else she possessed—and she could not lose Mairi's love for she had never had it.

As she stood there, she heard a commotion below her on the other side. She was so lost in her own sadness that she nearly did not move to look, but she heard her father's voice and crossed the room to see what lay below. Her uncle Felim and Mairi were just about to leave and were already seated on their horses in front of the great gates of the upper palisade. Her father walked towards them from the Hall with Fergus at his side. At a word from the Red King the boy ran over to his cousin Mairi. He held a package wrapped in skin.

"Here, Mairi," he cried in his clear voice, "I have a parting gift for you. See, I will put it in your saddle bag for you." He was so quick, and Mairi so taken by surprise, that he had already half-undone the bands that held the bag. Then—"No!" shrieked Mairi desperately, looking round at her father. "No! Give it to me and I will carry it myself."

By now the Red King stood beside his son.

"I think, my niece," he said, "that we will open up the bag. No, Felim, do not draw your sword unless you wish for your death."

Quite silently, the space around him had filled with the King's warriors and, after one short look, Felim resheathed the sword which he had half drawn out.

"Now, Fergus, open up the bag and see what you can find."

Grania watched as Fergus loosened the last band and drew the missing diadem from the bag while Mairi, grey with terror, sat still upon her horse. For several long seconds, her father looked in silence at his brother, then he motioned his nobles to gather at his back and his son to take up his position at his right hand. He took his great double-bladed sword from its scabbard and placing the point upon the ground, he stood with his two hands clasped across the hilt. As Grania watched him, he seemed to grow in size and strength, his red hair glowing in the sun that glittered on his golden ornaments and drew blinding brilliance from his naked sword.

She drew in her breath. This was her father, the King. His smallest word was law, and death, and should he turn the sword blade upwards, her uncle and cousin would be dragged away to die. He began to speak very quietly:

"You know, Felim, that by the laws of fosterage I should kill her because she has robbed the house that reared her and also by the old law of the Gathering because she has stolen in the Peace."

Felim stared at the ground, and the silence was broken only by Mairi's wild sobbing. Grania felt the sun warm on the wood of the window beneath her hand, and time seemed to hang suspended in the bright air. Then the King continued:

"But you are my youngest and my dearest brother and for all that has been between us, I will spare your child." He broke off as Dermot approached him with two arrows in his hands. They spoke together and, when the King looked up, he was in a towering rage. "So," he shouted, "so! To your mind it was not only the Circlet of Deirdre but the very Crown of Connacht that rested upon the wrong head. The King's Candle burns in the wrong Hall." He held up one of the arrows. "This one was most treacherously shot to kill me, or my son, and when I set my men to find its fellows, where then do they lie? In the quiver on my brother's back!" He thrust out his red head and glared at Felim, his face working, and his hands moving on the hilt of the sword. "Traitor!" he roared. "Traitor, that I have loved too much. What do you say of this?"

Felim spoke for the first time. His voice was thin and high. "I have much support for what I do," he cried defiantly. "Since I did not succeed as I tried, I will ride home to rouse my tribe to war. For 'tis said your mother was not our royal father's lawful wife, and so I claim—"

" 'Tis said," roared the Red King, " 'tis said! When 'tis said by me, then will I listen but not before. You are but an old crone mouthing above her dying fire. Begone, Felim! Begone, and take your thieving daughter with you. You have placed the naked sword between brother and brother of our tribe, and there it may well lie for years to come. Now go to your village and I tell you stay there, for if you come across my path again, you will find my mercy ebbed. Now get you gone!"

The gates opened behind him, and Felim turned his horse, lashing it with his spurs so that it leapt into a gallop, while his daughter and attendants were left to follow on as best they might. The huge gates crashed shut behind them and Grania watched her father stand for a long moment, then, sheathing his sword, turn and limp alone into the Hall.

Chapter V

After the Gathering, the quietness of ordinary life fell
heavily on the village and the fort. Grania was restless;
for a long time now she had not been allowed to ride abroad in
the forest in case she should be taken by marauding Normans.
She had to be content with riding and exercising her beautiful
Macha over a course of jumps her father's men had made
for her in the fields below the village. But since her wild ride
through the forest to Athenmore, she had not been so patient.

"I beg you, Father," she pleaded, "let me ride abroad again
with Fergus. We can take Dermot with us. You know the
Normans have not been within our lands for many months.
They are too busy with their building." Mischief gleamed
in her green eyes as she went on: "You know quite well that
lately you have had to go and look for the Normans when
you wanted to fight, for they have not come to you."

"So, cropped one!" Cormac twitched the short lock that,
for all Eithne's efforts, stuck out obstinately from her head.
"So, you speak thus to your royal father! But you speak the
truth. They were so taken up with building that I had to seek
them out to attack them and now my leg is healed, my son and
daughter, I will soon go and seek them once again."

"Oh, Father, must you?" Grania cried. "Your last dreadful wound has only just healed; can we not make peace like all the other tribes?"

Fergus lifted his face in scorn. "That is girl's talk, is it not, Father? I would wish to ride with you against the Normans were I older, come what may."

Grania wheeled upon her brother. "Girl's talk! Were it not for girl's talk you would still be fingering your numbers in the cloister! I only do not wish to see our father give his life when all the other chiefs and kings have thought the cause well lost."

Her father put his arm round her. "Come, daughter," he said, "me to my fighting and you to your pleasures. I tell you what, if Dermot will go with you, you may ride within the confines of Duncormac forest. But see you keep well clear of Athenmore and Ardrohan to the west."

"I would love to see Ardrohan and all those high-born lovely ladies," said Grania. " But enough that we may ride. Come on, Fergus, or Father may change his mind."

She gave her father a quick embrace and ran from the Hall and out into the misty day, with Fergus at her heels. This was one of those damp days that come in Ireland, when the light is drawn out of the sky to pour itself instead into the colors of the land. The grass on the hill glowed vivid green and the grey stone walls lay hard against it where the fields began. A haze of misty yellow seemed to hang about the trees and the mountains had drawn close, heavy and purple against the lifeless sky.

Grania lifted her face and sniffed the moist air, settling herself contentedly in her high saddle. She looked across at Fergus, who was fighting with his restless pony, and laughed. "I think, little brother, you have forgotten how to ride in your deep seclusion."

"And why not?" retorted Fergus. "You complain of being shut in, but at least you had Macha on the hill while I dared not even take the Abbot's nag round the courtyard. It is no wonder that I have forgotten, but let's go to the forest and I will soon remember."

For a long while they kept to the broad rides of the forest, letting their horses gallop as they would, aware only of the feeling of freedom and the damp wind on their faces. Dermot, his shouts unheeded, could only follow at their heels and pray that nothing would occur while they went so fast that he could not keep his eyes on them. At last, the children pulled up their horses at the end of a long, straight ride and, breathless, turned to wait for Dermot.

Against the soft green of the trees that were just bursting into bud, Grania's hair was bright as burnished gold. It lay in small damp rings against her flushed and excited face and was held in place by a fillet that glowed as richly as the hair itself. In the heavy air, the deep blue folds of her embroidered shawl hung down limply over her saffron *lenn.* The boy was fair in comparison with the rich coloring of his sister, and straight as a birch-tree. His thick, fair hair lay like a helmet to his shoulders above his speckled cloak of rough grey wool which the mist had beaded with crystal.

They laughed at Dermot as he came up and told him he was growing old.

"In faith, I am," he retorted, "but that is no reason for you to grow wicked. Your royal father said that you must stay with me. Now let us turn back into the forest and ride more quietly or we shall be within the Norman country."

They turned to the narrower paths and rode along gently beneath the overhanging trees. The horses' hooves were soft on the heavy moss, and Grania looked with pleasure at the little flowers that hid here in the depths of the forest, starring the ground under the trees.

But Fergus was watching something else. "Dermot," he said, "the moss lies very thick and does not hold much print, but don't you think that horses have been here recently?"

"Well done, my little master, you did well to notice it," Dermot said at once. "And you can see that there is something else to tell that man has passed this way."

Grania looked up from her flowers and the two children searched about them. It was Grania who saw it.

"See, Dermot, see! The trees are marked to make a trail that you can follow. Look, it begins to lead from this narrow path right into the pathless glades!"

"Let's follow it and see where it might lead."

"Dermot, please let us go. We'll not come to any harm."

Dermot was doubtful. The trail might lead to danger for it was too much to the west. But the children pleaded with him until he finally agreed to follow it for a way, so that they could get some idea of where it went, or who had made it. But once they started watching ahead for the marked trunks which led them through the most secluded glades, they forgot about following it only for a short way and went deeper and deeper into the trees. Dermot grew more and more anxious and more curious.

They had ridden for some time, when the brightness of the sky ahead told them that they were reaching the edge of the trees.

"The end of this journey had better be done on foot," said Dermot, and told them to tie their horses to a tree. The children were quick with curiosity as to what they would find when they reached the edge of the forest, as they crept cautiously behind Dermot, who suddenly stopped and drew his breath in a startled gasp.

"Merciful St. Patrick," he breathed, "it must be Ardrohan and I nearly walked you into it."

He would have turned and fled at once but the children held him and bade him wait until they had had a look. Afraid of noise, he could only agree, and they peered together through the boughs.

The trees ended where they stood and, before them lay a long stretch of flat green meadows shrouded with mist. Away to their right, a road emerged from the forest and circled off round the moated walls of the enormous castle that filled the sky at the far end of the meadows. There was a round tower at each corner of the mighty wall that faced them and they could just see the tiny moving heads of the sentries that patrolled behind their parapets. Above the walls was the inner fortress of the castle, the immense square keep, from the top of which floated a flag of scarlet, couched with gold.

"The Lion of England," whispered Fergus in an awed voice.

"Can you believe that their ladies have come all the way from France to live there?" asked Grania. "I would not like to live in it; it looks so bleak and cold."

"Who keeps it, Dermot?" asked the boy.

"De Courcy Rohan," answered Dermot, "one of King John's greatest barons who recently married his lady cousin. He is the highest Norman power that lies in Connacht. Come, in God's name, let us go. If your father knew where I had led you, I would not answer for my life."

They crept to their horses and rode back along the trail of marked trees until it led them across familiar paths; then they turned and made steadily for Duncormac.

Dermot was deep in thought. "It seems to me that we have found a Norman secret of some price," he said. "What, or who, do they bring into the castle by such a secret route?

What can't they trust to the road through the woods from Athenmore? I must speak to your father the moment we get back."

Grania looked at him out of the corner of her eye, and a mischievous smile quirked at her mouth. "And what then, Dermot, when he finds that you have led us to the very ramparts of Ardrohan Keep?"

"I must just risk it, my lady Grania. I think he will be so interested in what we have to tell him that he will not pay much notice to the way we found it out."

"I hope so for the sake of your neck, Dermot," Grania still teased.

Dermot smiled at her, a wry smile on his leathery, creased old face. He had served Red Cormac since his master was a young child and there was no one who could cross the King's path with greater safety; both Grania and Dermot knew this.

"Dermot," Fergus interrupted them, "since I was the one that first spoke about the horses in the wood, can't I be the one to tell my father?"

"Indeed, yes, my little master." The kindly warrior looked down at the boy. "I have no doubt your royal father will be as proud as I am that you have been so quick and in something so important."

As soon as he had handed his horse to a groom, Dermot made his way up to the Hall, followed by the two excited children. The Red King sat before a small table by the fire, his captains grouped around him, talking of his plans for the next assault upon the Normans.

He glared as the children entered the Hall. "What now?" he growled. "This is no time for children. Isn't it enough that you take away my senior captain when I need him for my council? Begone to your games and do not trouble me."

"Do not turn them away, sir," pleaded Dermot. "They have come on warriors' business, and I am well pleased with both of them. Let the prince tell you what he has discovered today."

The eyes of all the men turned upon the small fair figure, dwarfed against the King's candle at his side. He glanced round once. Then he held himself straight and started clearly on his tale. His father, who had faced him at first with plain indifference, was soon listening intently and, when the boy had finished, he whipped on Dermot.

"Is this so, Dermot?"

"It is, my king."

"You think it's some secret route into Ardrohan for things that are too precious for the forest road."

"I do. There had been many horses, not just one, and some heavy laden. It could have been a pack train."

A wide smile of pleasure spread across the face of then Red King, and he banged his fists on the great arm of his chair. "By the arms of Cuchulain," he cried, "if they require a secret track across the forest, we will give them one, hey Dermot, and one that will lead them to a warm welcome!" He grinned all round at his puzzled warriors. "We will restore the trees on the track that they have made and lay another. In the deep glades of the forest no one will ever notice where it changes. And the track that we shall make will lead them to where we lie in ambush; then we will see what this is that is too precious for the open road! What do you think of that?"

A shout of approval rose around the table and a few deep chuckles.

"Now," he continued, "there is a great deal to think about. Dermot, we will go together to the forest so that I can show you where I wish you to lead them. Then you will find the best woodsmen to obliterate their track and make the new

one—taking care that the new marks are treated so that they
don't look raw and fresh. There must be nothing that leads
them to suspect anything. We will arrange a signal for the
moment of attack—a troop of warriors cannot sit forever in
the woods and we may find we have some time to wait."

"May we come with you to the forest, Father? Please may
we come?" Both the children pleaded, but the King was firm.

"No," he said, "no, begone! You have done well, but this is
warriors' business now and you are only in the way. Begone!"

The two children were dismal as they left and they found
little consolation in watching their father as he rode away with
Dermot to the forest followed by two woodsmen in their short
cloaks and with their axes on their backs.

It was indeed a long wait. Fifteen tedious days had gone
before the signal of the woodpigeon's call was passed from
scout to scout across the greening forest. The King's House
Company of warriors who had stood alert all this time went
thundering from the fort, the Red King at their head. He was
happy to feel once more the weight of his great wicker shield
upon his arm and the heavy helm round his head.

On the palisades, the children waited. The long quiet hours
of the sunny day drew by and the forest lay green and secret
under the soft sky, telling them nothing of what went on within.
It was almost dark and the cool green evening light lay clear
above the mountains when, at last, they saw their father riding
from the trees.

"Oh," breathed Grania, "he is safe."

"And look, Grania," cried Fergus, "he has many laden
horses behind him. Dermot was right—it was a Norman pack
train. Come on Grania, let's see them in!"

They rushed down to the great gates, Grania running to her
father to kiss his hand as he passed through. The clattering

cavalcade threw up fine dust that hung about the riders like mist, muting colors and making the men unreal and strange in the evening air. The Irish warriors led the laden horses and, at the end of the procession, came a line of prisoners, still showing more surprise than any other feeling.

They were the first Normans that Grania had ever seen. She stared at them, at their unfamiliar clothes and cropped dark hair above their dazed and dusty faces. She saw one with a blood-stained bandage tied round his head.

"Why," she thought suddenly, amazed and pitying, "they are only people like ourselves!"

Fergus tugged at her arm. He was dancing with excitement. "Dermot told me 'twas a complete success! They only killed two. The rest laid down their arms in sheer surprise. Did you see the black-browed prisoners? I often peered at them from my windows at Athenmore. But come to the Great Hall, sister, for they will open all the bundle there."

He pulled her up the hill and Grania allowed herself to be led. Her mind was still on the bedraggled Normans. It was easy to remember that they were enemies until you saw them. And then? Her father had looked just the same when he was wounded. She shrugged off her confused thoughts as she came to stand beside her father's chair. The Hall smoked with new-lit candles and she watched the warriors cast the bundles on the rush-strewn floor in front of the King.

"Now, Dermot, cut them open," ordered Cormac.

From the first bundles, it seemed that the pack train had been meant chiefly for the ladies at Ardrohan. Grania gasped and could not help stepping forward, as the pack fell open to reveal the finest silks and velvets out of France, strange furs most beautifully cured, small shoes fashioned out of colored leather, skeins of softest silk for fine embroidery, and many other luxuries that raised only impatient cries from the surrounding men.

"These are not enough to cause such secrecy. Open the rest, Dermot," said the King.

"They are only small ones, sir," said Dermot, doubtfully, and did as he was told.

As he carelessly ripped open the first one, jewels poured out in a blazing river on his feet. The nobles gasped and Dermot gaped, his knife arrested in his hand. He went more carefully, spreading the bag open on a heap of shivering color hazed with light below the candles; every kind of jewel was piled together in one priceless mass.

"The others, Dermot," said the King.

All the small bags held either gold or jewels, and Red Cormac drew a long deep sigh of satisfaction when the last had been opened. He looked about him, his fine eyes glowing with excitement. "By the bones of Niall," he cried, "this was well done. I do not wonder that the Norman was so secret. He will miss this sorely! Now, come bring food and drink and let us feast to celebrate this day. Call the minstrels, let us sing! Let us make a song of how the Norman gave me all his jewels."

There was a babble of excited talk and exclamation as the nobles crowded round to stare and feel while Fergus pushed eagerly between their legs to gather straying jewels in the rushes.

Only Grania felt her heart grow still and cold with fear as Dermot, close beside her, spoke quietly to her father:

"Yes, my King," he said, "the Norman will miss it sorely. And from what I have heard of him, I do not think de Courcy Rohan will let it rest at that."

Chapter VI

De Courcy Rohan did not allow it to rest at that, but he let it rest so long that the Red King was lulled into a sense of false security, and he came to believe that the Norman had not found out who had robbed him. So when the avengers swept down upon Duncormac one brilliant summer dawn, the fort was taken by surprise.

There was an hour after daylight when the palisade gates stood open for the slow carts to rumble in and out with food and supplies for those within the fort. The Normans chose this hour to thunder out from the forest with horns and trumpets blaring. They pounded up through the startled village, tossing torches to set the dry thatch blazing on the huts.

The horns flared around Duncormac, and the warriors tumbled from their huts to rush unclad into battle; but the chance to close the gates was gone, and the Normans poured through the fort as the flames poured through the brittle timbers of the village huts. They waited for no gates at the second palisade, but attacked the wood with axes, breaking it before them by the pressure of their horses. The Irish fought like furies to prevent them, but in their haste, they were only half armed and most of them were on foot because they could not reach the stables.

Grania had left her bower when the attack began and was about to go into the Great Hall to find her brother or her father. She heard the horns and trumpets and the screaming of the women in the village, rising shrill above the thundering hooves and the deeper shouts of the men. As she stood motionless for one long helpless minute, she saw the first black smoke writhing above the palisades against the pearly sky. Then the use came back into her legs and she raced frantically for the Hall. As she crossed the court, the noise grew closer and, beside the clash of swords, she could hear the crackling of the wood while the sharp smell of smoke caught at her breath. She rushed through the door, crashing into Fergus, who was running out with Eithne at his heels.

"Where is my father?" Grania gasped.

"He is not here," said Eithne, adding urgently, "now, with all God's speed, I beg you children come with me."

"My father!" Fergus shouted, turning here and there in confusion.

"Your father cannot heed you now! Come, I beseech you, come with me! I know the fort is short of warriors, we cannot expect help from anyone." She dragged at Fergus's arm.

He turned reluctantly and was about to follow her and Grania, when a torch came flying over the upper palisade and landed in the thatch of the big hut beside the Hall. It. burst at once into flames.

It must be very dry, thought Grania stupidly, then, "Eithne!" she screamed. "The Book of Gospels! We must save the Holy Book! The guard has left his post."

She was right. Like every other man in the fort, the warrior guarding the Gospel Book had rushed downhill towards the fighting and now the roof of the hut that held his precious charge was burning fiercely.

Eithne grabbed Grania. "No!" she screeched above the roaring flames and the din of the battle that grew closer every minute. "You are more precious to your father than any Holy Book. Leave it alone and COME!"

But Grania tore herself from Eithne's grasp and rushed into the blazing hut. Eithne stood desperate. Should she follow one child or stay with the other? Already the palisades across the court were bulging to the Norman pressure.

Even as she hesitated, Fergus cried, "I cannot leave my sister like this," and, before Eithne could lay a hand on him, he had rushed after Grania into the blazing House of the Holy Book. Eithne could only follow at his heels.

Inside, Grania could see nothing and she was choked by the thick smoke. But from the time she could first take steps she had walked into this hut to touch the Holy Book and marvel at its beauty, and she needed neither sight nor breath to reach it. Steadily, she stepped across the room, fighting the panic that rose up within her as she heard the roaring flames above her head and felt the scorching heat upon her skin. Particles of burning thatch came drifting down like glowing snowflakes to light upon her hair and in her clothes and, try as she might to hold her breath, the smoke crept down her throat and parched her aching lungs. Still with her eyes closed, she took the book and turned, staggering with the weight of the jeweled case in which it lay. She made for the door and blundered into Fergus, who was coughing and gasping in the smoke.

"Out," she croaked, "out!" The smoke filled her tired lungs as she opened her mouth to speak and her head swam in the roaring gloom. As Eithne dragged them both through the doorway, the roof fell in upon the hut and the flames took greedy hold upon the wattle walls.

There was no time to wait now. As Grania gasped deep, frantic breaths of air and Eithne beat the scorching patches on her clothes, she saw that the palisade had been breached and that the court was full of fighting men. For one short moment, she saw her father with his shawl in ribbons down his back and blood on his yellow sleeve. His red head was uncovered and his great sword flashed as he swung fiercely at a tall man on a white horse that shied in wild terror at the leaping flames.

Eithne pulled her away. "Run, in God's name, run!"

They rushed down the side of the Hall and in among the scullions' huts behind it. There Grania stopped. "Eithne," she said hoarsely, "I cannot carry the Holy Book. It is too heavy and yet I dare not lay it down."

Eithne snatched the jeweled casket from the child and un-did the clasps to take out the small ordinary leather book. She threw aside the casket and thrust the book at Grania, pulling her down to where a serving boy waited anxiously beside a hole that he had hacked in the stout wood of the palisade.

"Mercy," he said, "you have come. I thought that they were lost." He pushed the children through the hole in the wood and Eithne after them.

"Thank you, Donal," she gasped.

This was the servants' quarter of the fort and the fighting lay around the other side. They slipped between the small huts and through the wicket in the middle palisade and raced down the slope behind the stables as the shouting and the clash of swords drew nearer. Mercifully, the high wicket was open and in another moment they stood outside the fort. Grasping a child in each hand, Eithne hurtled down the slope towards the woods. As the Normans had attacked on the long rise through the village, all was still quiet on this steeper slope and they gained the shelter of the trees without difficulty.

They stopped a moment and looked back. Smoke and flames rose from above the walls of the fort and from the walls themselves, making a pillar of tortured color against the pale morning sky, while the fierce crackle of burning timber almost drowned the noise of the battle. The lower palisades were blazing fiercely and a tongue of hungry flame licked round the upper one, feeding on the dry wood like a greedy animal. As they looked, a fresh surge of flame burst from the roof of the King's Hall.

Eithne grasped them both again. "They will be searching out the woods for those who have escaped. We must not wait."

She led them into the forest, avoiding the paths, and taking them through the thickets of bushes and long grass that lay between the trees. Although she pushed a way for them, the children found it very hard and stumbled ceaselessly on the uneven ground. They were torn by the thorns and struck by branches that whipped into their faces when they could not hold them back, and Grania was hampered by the Holy Book which, for protection, she had wrapped in the long ends of her cloak and held awkwardly beneath one arm. Before long Fergus was exhausted and on the edge of tears. Eithne took him and led him by the hand, holding the strongest branches from his way, while Grania followed as best she could.

When the high sun told her they had been battling for many hours, she begged for a rest. "Eithne, I can't go much farther unless we stop a moment. Tell me, do you know where we are going, or are we simply running anywhere?"

Before she would answer, Eithne made them creep into a deep thicket where they lay on the ground beneath the leaves and spoke in whispers.

"We have moved so slowly that we haven't really traveled very far and I am afraid that we may yet be found," she said.

"However, we will rest a little and then go on to where I know a stream to quench our thirst. There you can have a longer rest." Then she answered Grania. "No, my little mistress, we are not just running, I do know where we are going. There is an old hermit's hut in the heart of the forest that will give us shelter for the night. It is not so great a distance but I daren't approach it by the paths. Actually, it is so well hidden that there *are* no paths for quite a distance round it. That is why I chose it."

"How do you know the way then?" asked Fergus doubtfully.

"My mother was a very holy woman and she often came to visit the old man who lived here," said Eithne. "She used to bring me for company. The woods have grown over a great deal since those days but I can find the way by the sun."

Grania said nothing. If her father escaped, she felt sure she knew where he would go, but it was too early to say this to Eithne. When Cormac had recently shown her the secret hiding-place of the tribe, he had told her never to use it or tell of it to anyone unless she was desperate. She was not yet desperate and they might find her father on the morrow and all would be well. She followed Eithne obediently.

They went on, and soon, as Eithne promised, they came to a stream where they had a drink and then crept once more into the undergrowth to rest. Eithne produced a little bread which she gave to the children. Fergus complained that it was not enough.

"I know, I know," soothed Eithne, "but we are fortunate to have this much. Now sleep for a while and then we will go on."

Only Fergus slept but he slept long and deep and, when he woke up, the sun was well past its height. Eithne got up at once and hastened them on their way. She was afraid that they had delayed too long, and, through the long, late afternoon,

they battled with the forest—the green flowering forest that
Grania had always loved but that had today turned itself into
a cruel and exacting enemy.

Dusk was falling by the time they reached the hermit's hut
and to Grania's tired eyes it looked no different from many
other heaps of tangled creeper through which they had pushed
their way during the day. Eithne thrust the stems aside, however, and forced her way in, letting the weary children sink
down on the floor. She pulled the creepers and the branches
back across the doorway so that the hut might still be overlooked if, by any chance, the Normans got this far.

Despite all his efforts to be brave, Fergus began to weep.
He was only seven and he was tired and hungry and utterly
confused. Until today, the battles with the Normans had been
only an excitement, too distant from his happy life to matter
even when he was living in the monastery. Now the war had
come to his own home with fear and fire and death. Things
had happened to him so swiftly that there had been no time
to feel afraid; now he thought of his father and his home.
He thought of the warm fire in the middle of the Hall and
the friendly way it shone between the curtains of his bed.
He thought of the rough, loving bodies of his two great wolf-
hounds who always slept beside him so that he could lean
against them and rub his hands in their long tawny hair when
he woke up. He wept for loneliness and loss.

"Hush, hush!" said Eithne, gathering him to her side. "The
heirs to the thrones of kings must never cry." Her heart sank
within her as she spoke, and the thought came to her that this
forlorn small boy might no longer be his father's heir. It was
all too possible that the King of Connacht, himself, lay by her
side within her sheltering arm. She went on speaking as cheer-
fully as she could. "I was very clever," she said. "As I ran for

you, I reached out to the table in the Hall and see—" From the pouch round her waist she pulled out a piece of meat. "I did not tell you earlier, as I thought it was better that you should eat it now. We have no need to be hungry and we need only rest here for tonight. The Normans will not want to stay abroad in Morann country after what has passed today. They will search a little and go home. In the morning I think it should be safe to use the paths and we will go back to the fort to try to find your father. If we can't find him, then I shall take you to my family at Athenmore until we can."

"But won't the Normans find us there?" asked Fergus, Eithne smiled in the dusk. "The Normans *think* my father has made peace with them. His home is undisturbed and I shall say that you are my own two children who have lost their father in the raid on the fort."

As soon as she had spoken, she regretted the words she had chosen and looked sharply at Grania. But Grania listened quietly. She did not have to be reminded that the King's daughter did not cry; but Eithne's cheerful talk about her father did not deceive her. She ate her meat obediently, sitting quite silent beside the little door and staring through the creepers at the gathering dark. She lay down on the earthen floor with Fergus when Eithne told her to and wrapped the shawl around her, promising that she would do her best to sleep. Even in the sheltering darkness she did not cry, but neither did she sleep. She lay staring into the dark, her father's treasured book between her hands, steeling herself as best she could against the old familiar tales that Eithne whispered to her drowsy brother.

Chapter VII

In the morning, Eithne thought it safe to take Grania and Fergus by the paths and they made their way back through the forest to the fort, pausing only to drink at the stream and eat the fragments of their meat. All the way, they watched most carefully, not only for the Norman soldiers, but for any other people of the tribe who might be hiding in the forest as they were themselves. But they saw no one; and, by early afternoon, they had reached the forest edge below Duncormac.

Fergus was very quiet, feeling, perhaps, an echo of the sick terror that held his sister at the thought of what they might discover on the hill. Despite all Grania's pleas, Eithne forbade them both to leave the shelter of the woods in case there were still any roving men-at-arms around the fort. She herself, she said, would go on up the hill and see what she could find. But Grania was impatient; she wanted to see for herself what had happened to her home and, as soon as Eithne had left them, she grasped Fergus by the hand. Although she said nothing, he knew what she wished to do and, in silence, they walked out together to the forest edge.

It was another day of gentle Irish summer, the soft clouds idled in the mild sky and the flower-starred grass on the Hill of Duncormac was green and glowing in the sunlight. Upon this quiet colored scene was laid the blackened desolation of the village and the fort. The huts of the villagers were heaps of ash, and along the ruins of the great white palisade, a blackened post stood here and there above the cindered heaps that marked the buildings of the fort. At the very top, stood the tumbled timbers that had held the King's Great Hall, now laid bare by the burnt-out palisades, and around them were the shapeless mounds that had been the family home. There was no sound upon the hill. A few lazy trails of smoke still rose into the quiet air and the deathly stillness was marked only by Eithne's plump figure moving slowly up the slope upon her terrifying task.

It was more than Grania could bear. Daughter of the King or not, she sank down upon her knees, laid her face down in the scented flowering grass to weep bitterly and call hopelessly upon her father. Fergus knelt beside her and begged her not to cry, fighting back his own tears with the thought that had come to him as he stared up at the ruin on the hill. He now knew that he might well be Connacht's King.

He turned at a sound behind him and so was the first to see the two horsemen riding from the woods. At his urgent cry, Grania raised her head. The leading rider was a tall man—As tall as my father, thought Grania—riding a beautiful white horse caparisoned in colored saddle cloth and harness with, here and there, the gleam of gold and jewels. The sunlight dazzled on the rings of his chain mail and splintered off the brilliant metal of his round helmet. A richly worked clasp of gold held his embroidered cloak around his throat, and the jewels shimmered from the scabbard of his sword.

Grania got slowly to her feet and stood beside her brother. She, herself, was more dazed than frightened for such magnificence was seen only on state occasions, even in her father's wealthy court.

As the children stood silent, the stranger spoke. "Well then," he said, "and who are you?" His eyes below the heavy helm were dark and kind and he spoke to the children gently but a little awkwardly as though he found the language difficult. The children stared, but neither of them spoke, for there was something in the splendor and the presence of this man that made them speechless. Then the second horseman thrust himself forward. He was a heavy man, coarse and brutal, and clad in studded leather with a great axe swinging at his saddle.

"Answer!" he roared at the children. "Answer, you witless Irish brats. Do you not know who speaks to you? Answer Sir Jocelin, or, by my soul, I'll . . ."

The knight held up a quietening hand and the man subsided, growling into silence. By now Eithne, seeing what had occurred, had rushed back down the hill, and stood beside the children.

"You, girl," said the Norman, "can you tell me who they are?"

"Oh," Eithne was breathless from her haste, "my lord, they are but my own two poor children, country children from the village who lost their father yesterday in the raid upon the fort." She fell upon her knees with frightened tears rising in her eyes. "My lord, I beg you mercy. Spare my children, I care not for myself."

The Norman smiled. "Get up, girl, and stop your crying," he said. "I swear you keep your children well for a poor country wife. Your daughter's hair is bound with gold; your son has jewels in his collar and his cloak is held by a royal brooch. Come now and tell me who they are."

Eithne hung her head and Grania stepped forward. The tears were still lying on her cheeks, but, with Fergus at her side, she lifted up her chin and faced the Norman knight.

"My lord," she said clearly, "we greet you. I am Grania, daughter to my brave father Cormac. Should my father be alive, this then is Fergus, his son. If he is dead, my brother stands the King of Connacht."

"So-o-o-o," said the knight in long-drawn interest, but he had no chance to speak further, as the red-faced man rose roaring in his saddle.

"The Devil's spawn!" he bellowed. "The Devil's spawn themselves. Kill them! Kill them at once, I say! Kill them now!" He clawed at his great axe, his red face dark with hate and rage.

"Peace, Guilbert, peace!" the knight said patiently. "Since when have I waged war on helpless children when I can avoid it." He looked up at the ruin on the hill with sadness and regret upon his face; then he turned to Grania. "Your father lives, my child," he said. Fresh tears poured down Grania's face. "Not even I could hold him," the knight went on. "He fought his way out of the village, but we lost him in the woods, and do not know where he is. He is a noble fighter, and I am sure I should find him an equally noble friend if he could be thus persuaded."

Hope had flared up in Grania's heart. If her father had once got away, then there was every chance he might be safe, and she knew where. Please God this knight would ask no questions as to his whereabouts.

The Norman was speaking now to Eithne. "You have a home nearby, girl, or did you live in the village?"

"Yes, my lord. I served the Red King, but my father is Turlough Dhu of Athenmore, cousin in blood to Cormac."

"If I let you go to your home, you could, perhaps, in time send a message to the Red King?"

Eithne was cautious. "Perhaps, my lord," she said doubtfully.

A faint smile flickered across the dark face of the Norman. "Well, if perhaps succeeds, I bid you tell him that I have his children. They are not hostages and no harm shall come to them no matter what he does; but within my walls they shall live in safety." He looked up once more at the village. "And when he talks of peace, then so do I, and he shall have his children back. Tell him I give especial care to Connacht's future king." He looked keenly at Fergus, who lifted up his head and met him fairly glance for glance, but turned away confused as the man's appraising stare changed suddenly to warm amusement.

Then it was time for Eithne to leave them and a man-at-arms was summoned from the troop within the woods to see her safely to her home at Athenmore. She kissed the children fondly, especially the proud and unwilling Fergus, who felt himself too old for such caresses.

"I think I leave you in safe hands," she said. "Be good and dutiful and never for one moment forget your father. I shall see that he has news of you and then he can decide what he must do."

She bade them goodbye and climbed on the horse behind the soldier. As Fergus watched her go, it was all he could do to hold his lip between his teeth and stop himself from crying. Grania was already ashamed that she had wept before these Normans, and she now held her head high and waved bravely to Eithne until she was out of sight. Then she turned back to the knight, only to find her pride ebbing under the warmth and pity of the smile with which it also regarded her and her brother.

"I think you had both better ride with me," he said. "I don't trust Guilbert; he might lose you on the way."

He leant down from his saddle and swung first Grania and then Fergus before him on his charger. And so, astride the great white horse of Sir Jocelin de Courcy Rohan, the children set out for the castle which in the early summer they had surveyed so gaily through the trees.

As they rode along the woodland paths, the knight talked to them in his halting way of the little things about the woods, asking them to tell him of the trees and how to say their Irish names. Eventually he brought a reluctant smile even to the small, proud face of Fergus. They emerged on the forest road before the castle which they had peered at from the woods. Both of them turned to try to place the spot where they had stood with Dermot but neither of them spoke of this memory. The road curved round the castle in a mighty sweep and led up to the bridge that spanned the moat. A horn blared from the troop of men behind them and, for the first time, the children heard the long descending whine as the heavy drawbridge fell across the moat, followed by the screech of the great barred metal gate that was raised above their heads to let them through. The hooves of Sir Jocelin's white charger rang with a hollow clatter on the drawbridge, and then Grania and Fergus were within the Castle of Ardrohan.

The knight did not draw rein in the immense yard that faced them, lined with huts and stables under the great walls; he rode across the middle of this yard to where another draw-bridge spanned yet another moat, flanked also by two watch towers, as was the bridge outside. The bridge was already down, and Grania noticed that Guilbert and the men-at-arms halted in the outer yard, and only Sir Jocelin's squire with his standard rode before him across the inner bridge.

They were now below the enormous keep which was built upon its mound within this inner yard. A curved path led up the mound to an arched doorway where a soldier stood. Sir Jocelin rode on round the keep and, as he turned along the other side, Grania gave a gasp of pleasure. This side of the mound was laid out as a garden, with the slope beneath the grey stone keep a blaze of flowers confined between sweet-smelling hedges, and scattered here and there with seats of stone. A flight of broad stone stairs led from the garden up the wall to where a wide door opened in the upper storey. As Sir Jocelin's squire helped the children to the ground, a woman ran out from this door, her long blue skirts gathered in her hand and a white veil flying behind her from the circlet that held it on her long, black braided hair. Laughing and calling to her husband, she ran down the steps to meet him in the middle of the garden. Here Sir Jocelin embraced her fondly, forgetting the bewildered children who stood behind among the flowers.

Then Sir Jocelin turned and, coming back, he took them by the hand. "I will present you to the Lady Blanche, my wife," he said. "She cannot speak to you because she knows only French, but you will find that she is kind, as she is beautiful, and soon you will begin to understand each other."

He led them up to the lady and spoke to her swiftly in French. She answered him in amazement as she looked at the two children and her gentle face showed pity. Then she smiled and spoke soft words that they did not understand but which they knew for kindness, and put an arm round each of them. She looked troubled as she felt the rigid and unfriendly shoulders of the little boy but he followed quietly as she led them on up the wide stone stairs.

The big door led straight into a Hall, a little larger than their father's but, Grania thought, nothing like so beautiful.

The beams across the roof were plainest wood, and embroidered cloths, which the children later learnt to know as tapestries, were hung upon the dark stone walls. The tables and the chairs were rough and plain, and the fire burnt strangely in one wall with no apparent hole to take the smoke. The Norman castle looked a rough and barren place after the gilded richness of Red Cormac's Hall, with its carved and painted beams, its plastered walls most finely decorated and its vivid shields that hung above the carved and gilded chairs. Grania's thoughts must have lain clearly upon her face for Sir Jocelin turned and smiled at her.

"Do not despise us so, my little Irish maid. I know the wonderful beauty your land produces in the way of art, but be patient for we are newly built and built for war. When we have time to build for peace, we may yet leave much behind us that is beautiful."

The lady shepherded them to a table set in front of the fire and sat beside them as they ate. For all that Fergus muttered, "Norman food!" he ate it with a will, while Grania, eating more slowly, took time to watch the lady by her side. Her beauty took her breath away. Used as she was to the red and gold of Irish beauty, Grania was enchanted by this dark and lovely stranger whose great black eyes smiled at her from a face so delicate in color that she longed to touch its softness and to run her hands along the thick black braids of hair that fell below the Lady Blanche's waist.

After they had eaten all they could, they were bidden to speak with Sir Jocelin, who sat apart in a great chair of padded leather that was set in one of the deep windows. Enormous dignity lay in his very stillness and his voice was quiet as he spoke to the children. His gentle voice is always listened to, just as is my father's thunder, Grania thought.

Now he said, "I wish to speak with you so that we can understand each other. I want you to know that you are not prisoners in the usual sense. I simply say that you are safer in my home until your father feels he can make peace, and he and I, between us, can settle up this one rebel state. Do not think, my bantling Fergus, that I wish to put him off the throne of Connacht. Were all Ireland ruled as your father has ruled Connacht for these last six years, then, surely she would have more peace within herself. I wish your father to be King and that we may meet in peace. To this end, I promise you that I shall work; and, while you are with me, I hope that we may work together so that when your father claims you once again, he need have no shame in what the Norman has made of his children. Now tell me: is there anything that troubles you with which the Lady Blanche or I can give you help?"

Grania unfolded the bundle she had never ceased to keep protected in the corner of her shawl. "My lord, if you would keep us safely for our royal father then I beg you also to keep for us the holy treasure of his tribe. I took it from the fire before we left the fort and would feel it safer in your keeping."

Sir Jocelin took the ancient leather book and eyed it doubtfully until he opened it. Then his face broke into delight at the colored pages that flashed with gold as he turned them through his hands.

"This is indeed a treasure," he breathed, "and by whom . . . ?"

"By Columba himself, my lord. It is the greatest treasure that our tribe possesses. It means much to our people."

Sir Jocelin looked at her. "I understand it is important, Grania. I regard it no more a prize of war than I do you. My goldsmith shall find a casket for it where it may lie with honor until your tribe can hold it once again. Will that suffice?"

"I thank you, my lord. And may I and my brother feel that we are free to handle it, for we were brought up on its beauty and it is all we now have that means home to us."

"But certainly. Now I can see that you are both very tired. The Lady Blanche will take you to your rest. Whenever you wish to, we can talk together." His friendly smile lit his dark eyes and, for the first time, Grania smiled back shyly, feeling strength and safety in this soft-spoken man just as she had in her tempestuous father. Fergus, who had been preparing a speech of high defiance, was utterly confused when there was nothing to defy and, turning, he followed his sister without a word.

Chapter VIII

The long summer days drew by and rushed through windy autumn to the damp Irish winter, when the pale mists hung about the moat and the last of the wet, brown leaves slipped off the forest trees. The cold and darkness of the shortening days crept into the great castle, and the stone rooms, which had been cool and airy in the summer, grew chill and gloomy, despite the roaring fires and the blazing torches that hung on the sweating walls. The children now wore Norman clothes. Grania struggled with the long, full, hampering skirts, and the Lady Blanche gave them each a tunic of soft colored leather lined with fur against the winter cold. Grania smiled at hers with pleasure and smoothed the fine skin beneath her fingers, but Fergus snarled and sneered at all things Norman and said he would wear it only because he had no other choice.

"My brother," said Grania, as they sat together in their solar, a brazier at their feet and the bright new tunic thrown down on the floor, "I think you only harm our cause by your ungraciousness. Our father would not wish you to behave like this; he would want you to show the Normans dignity and courtesy when they have you quite fairly in their power. For,

remember, there was nothing to prevent Sir Jocelin from kill-
ing us—as Guilbert would still do if he got the chance. But yet
Sir Jocelin brings us up as his own children so that you may be
ready to sit upon the throne of Connacht. And all you have to
show him is your churlish face and your discourteous tongue."

Fergus turned on her, his fair face dark and sullen. He was
now over eight years old and, in these months at Ardrohan,
he seemed to have grown a great deal older. Grania could not
believe he had ever been the frightened child who had wept
so sadly in the hermit's hut.

"What use is it," he demanded now with bitterness, "a
throne of Connacht from which the Norman rules, even though
I might hold the name of king?"

"That is what our father thinks," answered Grania, "but I
live daily in the hope that he may change his mind. I feel that,
if only he could meet Sir Jocelin, he might well see things in a
different light. I think they are both so noble that I can't imagine them disagreeing."

Fergus only grunted in reply, and Grania smiled at him. She
knew him well and was aware that he fought against affection
for Sir Jocelin and his lovely wife because he felt that loyalty
to his father and his tribe demanded hatred of the enemy and
endless talk of escape. "Although," he would mutter, "the
Norman sees to it that there is never any chance of *that*."

Gradually, he was being drawn into the life of the other
boys who lived within the castle. He took his lessons with
the nobles' sons and, against his will, his French improved
rapidly. Each day he took part more willingly in the sport and
pastimes that took place in the vast space beyond the ladies'
garden, which the children learned to call the Inner Bailey.
He ran and wrestled and learned to joust and tilt, and he was
always happy if he could win because he felt he proved his

Irish strength; but all the time he was confused and this made him haughty in case he should grow to like too much the boys with whom he fought. Sir Jocelin watched him and watching, smiled, and left him alone.

While Fergus tired himself with hating, Grania had learnt to love the Lady Blanche. Sir Jocelin's wife was very young, gentle, gay, and serene; Grania had never seen her otherwise. But for all her gaiety, she ruled the great household and the servants knew the strength of her authority. She had no children of her own as yet, and a deep affection had sprung up between her and her little Irish ward. She would have loved Fergus just as easily, had he permitted her, and she would merely raise her hands at his surly habits and laugh her quick French laugh.

The only consolation that Fergus found in his unhappiness was his father's Holy Book, which had now been housed in beauty and honor in a golden casket lit with jewels and placed upon a table in the Great Hall. During the months he had passed at Athenmore, the boy had been deeply interested by the arts of the monks, and he had sat, hour after hour, beside them in their little stalls along the cloister, watching and learning the great art of illumination. He also learned to read and print and paint himself, and to listen to the tales of the world that came back in the letters and stories and poems of the wandering Irish scholars. He missed all this greatly for, like his father, his hands were made for art as well as for the sword. By poring over the Holy Book, he could recover some of it, but he was too proud to ask for colors or for parchment so that he could try himself.

One day as he sat in a deep window of the Hall gazing at the art of Columba, Sir Jocelin came unnoticed and sat down beside him.

"My lord," cried Fergus, jumping to his feet, and would have gone.

"Stay, my proud young Fergus. Do not always be in such a hurry to get away from me. Sit down and let us talk about the Holy Book. You like it much—I see you read it often."

" I do, my lord." The boy's voice was stiff.

"Why?" asked the knight. "Is it simply that it is your father's?"

Fergus looked up into the man's face above him. The keen eyes holding his own seemed to read his thoughts and Fergus hungered for the kindness that lay in their depth, which he had resisted far too long. Suddenly it all came out; his love of color and of painting and the attempts the monks had let him make with colors and gold; the stories and poetry that he had learnt to read, all written by the scholars of his country; and his wish to try again to copy the beauties of the ancient books.

Sir Jocelin listened intently and when Fergus stopped suddenly, abashed that he had spoken so freely to the Norman, he made no move towards the boy but simply said, "I understand. But this castle is geared to war. We have our tutors for our children so that they will not lack schooling, but they come from France and England and cannot teach you what you want to learn. Leave it to me and I will think what we can do."

He got up and left Fergus looking after him. It was the first time he had talked freely with the knight and Sir Jocelin had not hurt his pride by making much of it, but had walked away. Next time it would be easier.

A few days later, Sir Jocelin summoned Fergus to him. "I have been speaking of your need for Irish learning and I have found that a hermit monk who seems to have all the arts that you want to learn, lives in the forest over by the sea. Once in every few years, he travels to the Abbey at Athenmore to get his colors and his books. I have said that we will bring him these, and much more frequently, if he will take you as his pupil. The forest is so wild in that direction that there are no villages for miles. I think it should be safe to let you go, escorted by a troop, once the dark winter days are over. But I would wish for your word on the Holy Book that you would not make your journeys an occasion to attempt escape."

Fergus stared at him, then at last he spoke. *"You* would do this for me! And you would *trust* me to leave the castle in this way?"

"Are you not a king's son?"

There was a long silence and Fergus bowed his head. "My lord," he said, "I think I had forgotten."

From that day onwards, Grania was glad to see her brother become his usual merry self and to hear his long clear laugh peal out as frequently now as it had done when he lived in his father's fort.

The Wreath of Advent had now been brought into the Castle Hall to mark the time until Christmas. Three tall candles stood within the wreath of bay and laurel and at dusk every day the Lady Blanche would light them, bidding all other lights to be put out. In the small soft glow, a prayer was said that Christmas might be blessed and then, with all the torches lit again, the people of the castle went on with their Christmas preparations.

There was frantic rushing in the kitchens as the Feast drew near, and cheerful parties of the men-at-arms were hurried to the woods to cut holly and laurel branches; the sweet-scented fir was brought in for the women and children to weave with bay and rosemary to make garlands for the Hall. By Christmas Eve, the keep was ready for the Christmas coming.

The garlands, hung on the wide beams of the roof, drooped above the waiting tables and the holly berries twinkled in the dancing firelight across the mighty chimney breast. The sharp sweet scent of the fir mixed with the tempting smells of cooking floating up from below and the excited children fingered the little bed of straw beside the fire that Lady Blanche had made to hold the Christ Child when He came. At dusk, before the torches on the wall were kindled, the blackened Advent candles were removed and the enormous Christmas candle was lit triumphantly in the middle of the wreath to burn each evening through the Feast.

The night was calm and starlit as they walked across the Inner Bailey to where the wooden church lay close beside the curtain wall, and, as Grania watched the Christmas play against the silver candlelight, she prayed and wondered for her father. She listened with half her mind to the music of the Christmas Mass and as she thought of previous Feasts when she had knelt beside him while his voice led the singing, the candles blurred and slipped before her eyes, and she dropped her head into her hands. But she forgot her sadness in the gaiety when Mass was over; all the children raced across the starlit Bailey and through the ladies' garden and clattered up the stone stairs into the Hall. Midnight was now past, and the Christ Child here and the gifts that He had brought lay about His little cradle on the rush-strewn floor beside the blazing fire. There was happiness and merriment, kisses and kind wishes and, on the laden tables, a meal for all which lasted long into the morning, when the exhausted children were coaxed away to sleep so that they would be ready for the merrymaking later in the day.

Christmas Day belonged to feasting and celebrations and the tables rocked beneath the dishes that followed in procession once the roasted boar had ringed the company. The tables were strewn with rosemary and set with plates of all the precious metals, vast dishes of fine carving and slender jeweled cups. The boar was followed by the beef; the roasted pig; the great mince pies; the roasted goose; and a peacock with its tail outspread upon the plate; the pasties and the pies; the pastries and the sweets; and the fine French marchpane that the children loved. The mummers and the jesters leaped in frolic in the center of the floor and the King of Christmas led their capers, his golden bells a-jingling on his scarlet tunic and his tinsel crown askew round the fool's cap on his head.

The greatest noise was where the crowd of children, bright as flowers in their Christmas clothes, were crouching at the huge log that filled the hearth, popping raisins in the glowing ashes and crying out their wishes.

"It is your turn, Grania. Place your raisin and you must tell us what your wish is if it should pop and grant it!"

"Grania, Grania. It is Grania's turn," cried the little dark-eyed Normans, and Grania put her raisin in the fire, jumping backwards from the glowing wood.

"Make your wish!"

Her face grew wistful in the firelight. How could she make the wish she wanted, for it was no part of children's play.

"Yes, I have wished!" she cried suddenly and, just as she spoke, her raisin popped and the children cried out to know her wish.

"It was an easy one," she said, "I knew it *must* be true. I wished that my father was thinking of us on this Christmas Day."

"Poor Grania, of course he will be!" the children cried and, heedless, passed on to another turn, but Fergus caught her eye and moved across to press her fingers with his own, although he never ceased to yell his loudest in the game.

At that moment a sergeant-at-arms came pushing his
way through the happy crowd that was now dancing to the
music of the minstrels in the gallery. He had a paper in his
hand. At last he reached Sir Jocelin in the dance and asked
to speak to him, but before the knight could answer he started
to pour out his tale. The dancing stopped and the gaily colored
crowd drew close to listen, the King of Christmas dropping
his tinsel crown upon the sergeant's head with cries of admiration,
and the children climbing up on the benches and shouting
that they could not hear. When everyone was silent the
man was asked to start again. It seemed that the sentries on
the castle walls had sounded the alarm because a man had
ridden from the forest road bearing in his hand the white flag
of peace.

"I' faith, my lord," the sergeant said, "I thought our troubles
were all over and this Irish chief had come to sue for peace."
Grania grasped Fergus so tightly by the arm that she all but
knocked him from the bench on which he stood. But no; another
man had ridden out, carrying a huge bow and, standing
beside the first man, he had raised it and shot an arrow at the
walls. The first had fallen in the moat and then the second,
but the third had cleared the wall and landed in the Bailey,
whereupon the men had turned and ridden back into the forest.
The sergeant had run from the ramparts and retrieved the
arrow from the ground within the Bailey, which had fortunately
been empty, with all the castle company inside at the
Christmas feasting. Bound round the arrow, he had found a
message. He gave the paper that he held to Sir Jocelin.

The knight looked at it for a moment and then smiled,
"There lies no message here for me," he said. "Come here,
my little Irish wards and read your letter. I understand very
little of it but enough to know that it is for you alone."

Many hands pulled the children forward and Sir Jocelin handed Grania the paper. She read it once with difficulty, for she found it hard to speak, but then she read it again, this time aloud to Fergus. It was short and in their own language.

"I send my blessing to my son and daughter on this Christmas Day, bidding them remember even through my longest silence, as I do remember every day, that they are mine. By the hand of their father, Cormac, King of Connacht."

Grania blinked away her tears and looked at her brother, who stood very straight and still. Then he moved toward her and they stood alone together in the bright circle of the Norman crowd. His blue eyes blazing with delight, he gave his hand to Grania.

"Shall we dance, my sister?" he said.

Chapter IX

When the spring days came round, Sir Jocelin kept his promise, and it was arranged that Fergus should ride on two days in the week to study with the Irish hermit in the forest. Tired of the high grey wall round the Bailey, Grania sought Sir Jocelin and begged that she could go too.

"Please, my lord, let me ride with Fergus. I can learn whatever the good monk may have to teach, too, and it will help me for, quite honestly, I have almost forgotten how to speak my native tongue."

The knight smiled his wide, delightful smile. "Indeed? Poor Grania, I do pity you. Yet when I hear you talking in corners with your brother, it is not Norman French you speak, nor do you seem to find yourself at a loss for words! But you may go—and do not seek for excuses. You can go so that you can enjoy the freedom of the ride. I do not see that two of you, if well protected, run any greater risk than one."

"My lord, I thank you. I promise you I do not seek to escape."

Sir Jocelin laughed again and told her to go.

When Fergus had promised on the Holy Book that he would make no attempt to escape, he and Grania rode together from the castle. They passed beneath the great barred gate which

they had learnt to call the portcullis, and across the drawbridge to the soft green meadows, surrounded by a troop
of men-at-arms. This time they did not take the wide road
through the forest, but made across the open fields that lay
before the castle, entering the trees at the far side. The woods
were wild and overgrown, flushed with soft green leaves and
spattered with spring flowers.

"It was only by chance that we ever found this hermit,"
said Michael, the kindly long-faced man who led the troop,
"and he was most reluctant to be known. If we are going to
come this way all summer, then we must cut a better path. We
need not keep to the woods for long—soon we can skirt along
the fields above the sea."

The children were so delighted to be riding outside the
castle that they did not mind the narrow path and the jostling
horses and the tangled branches that whipped at their heads.

"Isn't Sir Jocelin afraid that my father or his friends might
be lying in these woods and try to rescue us, Michael?"

"No, my little Irish prince." Michael often talked about
his own son who had been left in England. He was exactly
Fergus's age and size and so the Sergeant always had a spe-
cial softness for the captive boy. "In all the years Ardrohan
has been built, we have never seen a living soul within these
woods, except the hermit, and he has sworn himself to secrecy.
The forest lies unbroken to the sea and we have found no
villages."

"Why is there a path then, Michael?"

"We ourselves made it to the sea. My lord plans later to
make a road so that we can have an entry to Ardrohan from
the water."

"You certainly make yourselves at home!" Fergus could
not help but jibe against the Norman conquest for all that his

opinion of Sir Jocelin was now as high as Grania's. Michael made no answer.

"Have you ever seen the sea?" he asked as the bright daylight ahead showed that they were coming to the border of the trees.

Yes, they had seen the sea. "Before the Normans came," said Fergus, clear and haughty, and Grania exploded into laughter for she knew very well that he could not remember such a time. "Before the Normans came and destroyed the customs of our country, it was my father's custom every year to move with all his people from Duncormac and go to spend the summer months in his palace on the flat lands by the sea or else in the soft hills to the west of Connacht."

Grania nudged him for his pompous words. "Peace, brother," she said crushingly, "you are not yet king."

Fergus collapsed in happy laughter, taking all the sting out of his words so that Michael laughed as long as they did.

They were now above the sea. The green fields lay along the edges of the forest, their brilliance broken by clumps of rock, half covered by the scrambling growth of pink and yellow flowers. The rocks grew more barren and more frequent as the fields sloped to the sea, until the clear green water foamed and crashed only on piles of jagged rock. The cavalcade rode on along the fields, stepping carefully between the boulders, until, suddenly, the woods fell back upon a clearing of stone-strewn grass. A flock of startled birds rose in front of them. Set against the forest was the tumbled ruin of a church. There was not much to be seen of the stones that had been used to build it, for ivy covered the jagged remnants of the walls and the naked edges where the stones had fallen were softened by a fringe of grass.

"Oh!" Grania exclaimed, "what a gentle, friendly place, with the forest and the flowers and then the sea in front. I am glad that we will come here often."

Michael bade the troop tie up their horses and arranged them round the open space so that it was guarded on all sides. Then he led the children to the ruin and they climbed through a broken arch to the inside of the ancient church. On a fallen stone in the middle of the grass, a monk was sitting and, as the children came in, he turned and smiled at them. His old face was wise and mild and his eyes so full of friendship that they instantly smiled back.

"You have sent my friends away," he said in a regretful voice.

The children stared at him, puzzled.

"Wait," he said, "wait quietly and do not speak."

The children looked at each other but they did as they were told, their eyes on the tranquil face of the old man. In a moment there was a whirr of wings and a bird flew down to light upon the hermit's shoulder, to be followed by another and another until a ring of birds were sitting all round him on the grass; even a seagull hovered, and eventually came to rest between his feet.

"Keep you still," the hermit said. "They have no fear of man for I have taught them love; but now they have too many people and they do not understand."

The children watched with fascination as the old man talked to all the birds round him and they seemed to understand and to hang upon his words.

Then Grania burst out excitedly, "My father told us . . ."

With a whirr and clatter of wings the birds were gone.

"Oh!" she cried, her hands flying to her mouth. "Oh, I do beseech your pardon."

"It is no matter," said the old man, "they will return. And we must go now to your brother's lesson. What did your royal father tell you?"

"He told us," Grania smiled with confidence at the lined and gentle face, "of a monk that lives beyond the seas. He has made the animals and birds his friends just like you and people say they even talk to him."

"Ah—the blessed Francis. I have heard of him at Athenmore. But now we will go to our lessons. Have you come also, daughter, to learn with me? My name is Brother Colman. If you will follow me into my cell, we will see what art and learning we can contrive to interest you, as your Norman lord commands."

So the pattern of the children's lives was laid down for the next two years. In the spring and summer they rode out to Brother Colman, and Fergus was happy in his growing skill with colors and brush. Both he and Grania were deeply interested, not only by the rich learning but also by the store of simple knowledge of the woods and fields that the old man had. On many days Grania did not sit with Fergus but would settle herself instead on the fallen stone in the middle of the grass and wait in silence for the birds to come; she was overjoyed when they settled at her feet or on her hands.

As each autumn came and the children knew that they would ride no more until the spring, they did their best to persuade the old man to let them make his life more easy for the winter—to bring him warmer clothes and better food against the cold. But he would have none of it; he said his needs were simple and that he only undertook this teaching for the sake of his King so that his son would not grow completely Norman in captivity. For the winter, Brother Colman said, he still sought peace and did not wish it to be broken.

So every year when the forest leaves grew golden and the autumn winds began to blow the tumbling sea to anger, the children bade goodbye to the monk and returned to pass the winter inside the castle walls. Fergus had his brush and color and clean parchment for painting and he gave himself up quite happily to working with his Norman tutors and taking part in the sports and pastimes of the castle. Grania, too, would attend her lessons and sit round the fire in the Great Hall or in the Lady Blanche's solar, practicing her French and working at the fine embroidery in which the Norman ladies so excelled.

But for all they seemed content, there was one thing, as time went by, of which the Irish children never spoke. "Through my longest silence," their father had said in that one Christmas message, but there had never been another word and the silence had grown so long that each of them secretly feared that their father would never have them back. It was not that they were afraid in these years that he was dead; on the contrary, they knew that he was very much alive, for news came frequently of some fresh outrage on the Norman pride; but no one knew from whence he came or where he vanished. Many times, on hearing news, Sir Jocelin had ridden out, hoping to waylay him, for he never seemed to have many men in his attacks, which were more for mischief than for damage. The knight hoped that he might surround him with a greater force and so take him without a battle and come to terms of peace.

But on each occasion Sir Jocelin came back with a baffled face. It appeared that the Red King could vanish with the wind and leave no trace. Each time, Grania hid her fierce relief and breathed a prayer of thanks that the knight had not thought to question her as to where her father might be hiding.

As long as their father harried the Normans, however, there could be no hope that he would have them back, and in this lay the children's grief. They knew that their father had to choose between them and his pride and, to Grania and Fergus, as time went by it seemed sadly obvious that he had chosen pride.

Chapter X

It was in the third spring when they had just begun to ride again to Brother Colman, that the pattern broke. Grania was now twelve years old and Fergus almost eleven, and their hopes of returning to their father and their tribe were growing faint. By this time Fergus was very skillful with his brush and loved his studies so that his visits to the monk were of great importance in his life. If, for any reason, he could not go—perhaps Sir Jocelin could not spare the troop for escort—he fretted for his lost lessons until Grania laughed at him.

"I' faith, brother," she would cry, "it seems I did the wrong thing ever to snatch you from the cloister."

One day when spring was drifting into early summer and the calm sea stretched green below the milky sky, they rode as usual along the fields to Colman's hermitage. Grania sat that day and read with Fergus, for the lesson interested her, even though the birds clamored in noisy flocks round the ruined church. But before the lesson ended, Brother Colman closed his book and turned to Grania.

"I wish, my daughter, to speak in private to your brother. Would you forgive me if I asked that you should leave us?"

Grania was surprised and puzzled as to what the monk could want with Fergus. The four walls of the hermit's world lay in these ruined stones and between the covers of his books and she could not think what kind of a secret lay there that he would want to talk about. However, she smiled agreeably and left them and went out through the noisy fluttering birds to sit with Michael on the stones above the sea.

The monk watched her go and then turned slowly back to Fergus, who sat waiting with inquiring eyes upon the old man's face.

"My son," said Brother Colman, "I have a message for the King of Connacht's heir. Are you willing that *you* should take it?"

As the words sank into his mind, Fergus grew so still, it seemed as though they were a spell that turned him into stone. But his thoughts were whirling. This was the moment he had hoped for all these Norman years. But could he seize it? In his journeys to the monk, he was tied by honor to the promise given to Sir Jocelin that he would take no chances to escape. Before he found his tongue, the old man spoke again.

"You are as doubtful whether you should take the message as I was doubtful whether I should give it. I know your promise to the Norman and I know, also, that he treats you well and does not deserve deceit. With myself, I had to argue as to whether I was first a monk who long since cut all worldly ties, or first an Irishman of your father's tribe whose duty lay with Connacht."

"What made you choose the second?" asked Fergus slowly.

"I prayed, my son, and I thought long in quietness. It seemed that I could do my duty best by giving you the message but never asking you how you would deal with it. I am but the vessel for the word to pass to you and back again. I take no part nor have any feeling as to what may result."

"Can you tell me more, good Brother," asked the boy, who was finding his speech again and recovering from the first shock of news he had long lost hope of hearing. "Can you tell me who brought this message and from where, and what is it that you want me to do?"

"I do not know who brought it. The man came by darkness and I never saw his face under his hood. Neither did he say from whom it came, directly, but led me to believe it was your father. From who else could it come? Who else would want to rescue you? He asked me to tell you of the plan. You are to name a day on which you will be in readiness and the spot is on the edge of the forest above the sea, opposite where the great rock rises from the water. There will be men hidden in the trees to take you from the Normans."

Fergus felt a wild surge of excitement but he kept his voice as calm as possible. "And what about my sister?"

"He did not mention your sister."

"And what if I should name a day, and then not come, as could happen only too easily."

"Then I imagine you would have to name another one."

Fergus sat with his mind in turmoil. "Brother Colman," he said at last, "I cannot decide this at this instant. There is a great deal to think about. I will give you an answer the next time we come."

"I think you are wise, my son. Such things are not decided in a moment. And will you tell your sister?"

"I don't think so, Brother. I know nothing yet, but give me time to think. If I don't tell her, then it will be the first secret that I have ever held from her. Let me go now and I will think about it."

"Go in peace, my son."

Fergus left the little stone cell built against one ruined wall and, walking through the arch and across the grass, he came out on the rocky shore. With half his mind, he saw his sister paddling barefoot in the shallows, her shoes and stockings had been left on the stones and her long blue skirts were gathered in her hands. The soldiers lounged about, taking their guard for granted after three summers of fruitless watching. They lazed idly in the warm sun, talking among themselves. Fergus took note of all this. The guard was but a formality now and any attack that came was almost certain to succeed by reason of being unexpected. At the thought of a successful rescue and of returning to his father and his tribe, even if it were in hiding, the boy could hardly keep himself from shouting his delight and crying out his news to Grania. But what of his promise to Sir Jocelin? His years at Ardrohan had taught him great respect for the Norman knight and the standards of loyalty and honor that he demanded. And his father would want him to be honorable, too. If he knew that Fergus had taken an oath upon the Holy Book, the last thing the Red King would want would be for him to dishonor it.

He ought to tell the knight about the message—but then, without a doubt, Sir Jocelin would stop his journeys to the hermit. At the thought of losing all the world of learning and interest that the monk had brought him, Fergus was seized with despair. He could not bear to spend his summers shut up in the castle as he did his winters. He could not possibly tell the knight if that was to be the result. What then should he do?

A voice interrupted his tangled thoughts. "Oh, Fergus, why have you got so long a face on such a lovely day? Has Brother Colman set you a very great task; so great that you can't face it?"

Fergus forced himself to smile at Grania, who had dropped beside him on a stone and was trying to drag her stockings over her wet feet. "I think, my sister, that is exactly true."

Michael came to call them to their horses and they rode for the castle. Fergus looked at the forest with new eyes, knowing now that it was no longer empty.

For the next few days he kept much to himself, trying to decide what he should do and where his duty lay. When they went to Brother Colman the next time his mind was clear. It was easy to talk to the monk without arousing suspicion, as in the lovely sunny weather Grania could not bring herself to go inside but stayed to talk to the birds and to play along the shore.

"Well, my son?" the old monk said when they were alone together. "Have you decided whether you are Fergus or the heir of Connacht?"

"Brother Colman," said the boy slowly and carefully, "I am always Connacht's heir, but my father would not wish me to place even that above an oath of honor. So I cannot take secret advantage of the knight to whom I gave my oath. On the other hand, I am also Fergus and my Irish lessons are very precious in my Norman life, although Sir Jocelin gives us so much. I cannot bring myself to tell him about the message for he would be certain to stop my coming here. So I have decided to do as you. I send no message and I take no part. If my father rescues me, then it must be without my help. In this way, I feel that I will not be breaking my oath."

Colman smiled gently at the boy as he ended his long and careful speech. "It may not be with your help, my son, but it will certainly be with your knowledge."

"I know, I know." The boy's face puckered with distress. "That nags at my conscience. But it is the best I can do," he went on almost petulantly, as if he had been asked too much. "I couldn't bear to be shut up for a whole year in the Norman keep and never to see you."

"Very well. It shall be as you say. When this man comes again, I am to say there is no message."

"Yes, if my father takes it that I have forsaken him, then I must bear it. If he still comes to rescue me, then it is nothing of my doing."

"And the Lady Grania?"

"I have not told her. It was too hard a matter to decide for anybody else to help me, even my sister. But if my father arranges for my escape, you may be sure that Grania will not be overlooked."

"So be it. Now, my son, we will continue with our lesson."

Chapter XI

Fergus now lived in happy fear. He could not believe that his father would take his silence to mean he did not want rescuing, and every day when they rode towards the ruin he hoped that it would be the end of his captivity. The fear lay in the fact that he had often heard Sir Jocelin say that his father's men were few, and the Normans were well trained and excellently armed, and might well have the advantage even if taken by surprise.

Day after day passed, however, and they rode to Brother Colman and safe home again into Ardrohan. Fergus knew that his message had been given, for the monk had told him that the Irish messenger had come again to ask for it, but there had been no word since. The strain began to tell on the boy, who did not confide his secret to anyone and each day faced disappointment when they cleared the forest and headed over the open fields towards the castle. He was beginning to think that his father had taken his silence to mean that he did not want rescuing; but there was always another day to ride and always the chance that it might be the day.

In the Great Hall he found Grania sitting by the fire, her embroidery in her lap.

"What, Grania, are you not ready to come with me?"

"Not in this rain, Fergus! Look out of the window. I do not thirst for knowledge quite so desperately as that."

Fergus stood at a loss for words. His mind was so filled with his own plans that he had forgotten all about the fickle Irish weather, had forgotten that on the frequent days of heavy rain, Grania stayed within the castle while he rode off by himself. Without attracting too much attention, there was nothing he could say that would either persuade her to ride with him or provide an excuse for him to stay at home. What if this should be the day? There was nothing he could do; he could only comfort himself by remembering how Grania loved the knight and Lady Blanche and by thinking, that, once he was with his father, they would contrive some way to get her out. He looked at her red head bent over her embroidery, and he suddenly lifted it and kissed her forehead.

"Goodbye, sweet Grania," he said.

"Oh," Grania laughed at him, "you do suddenly love me a great deal! But do not worry, I will see you at dinner, stuffed full of Brother Colman's knowledge."

Fergus laughed back. She was quite right; why should it be today, of all days? He left her and clattered down the winding stair in the corner tower and out through the crowded lower Hall to where a page waited with his horse beside the drawbridge to the Outer Bailey.

It was a wet and uneventful ride; the rain drove in their faces across the open fields, and the wet trees dripped heavily upon them in the woods. By the time they left the forest and came out above the heaving, sullen sea, the rain had stopped but the clouds were low and the day still dark and threatening. Fergus did not stay as long as usual, for he was conscious of the sodden soldiers waiting for him under the trees. Also he was disturbed by the fact that Grania was not with him and he was anxious to be back with her in the castle. So he put his wet cloak round him and bade Brother Colman goodbye. The men fell in about him with alacrity as he swung on to his horse. He breathed a long sigh of relief when they had passed the spot which had been mentioned in the message and the dripping woods continued silent and deserted. All would be well today, and in future he would think ahead to see that there was no danger of Grania being left behind.

He was so happy at having passed the point of danger that the ambush on the forest path caught him completely by surprise. At one moment the cavalcade was riding steadily along the track and, at the next, it had become a mass of struggling men, above which rose the terrifying yells of his own people entering into battle. The boy was riding near the leaders of the troop, between the men-at-arms, with only Michael in front of him. The Irishmen attacked on both sides from the forest but, with a flash of insight, Fergus realized that it was the sword on his right that was meant for him. Even as it descended, he looked into his uncle Felim's face and knew that he had been deceived. It had been no message from his father that the monk had brought but a plot to take the life of Felim's rival.

Faster than thought, Fergus flung himself sideways in his saddle and his uncle's long two-bladed sword cut down across the body of the Norman soldier who tried to intervene, gashing the boy's leg as the weight of the dying Norman threw him off his horse. Dazed and helpless for a moment, Fergus crouched among the flying hooves, putting his hands up to protect his head. Then he saw that his horse's reins were still looped round his wrist, and he scrambled to his feet. One hasty glance showed him that Michael held his uncle hotly engaged.

"Follow me, Simon, FOLLOW ME!" he yelled to the soldier nearest him and, hurling himself onto his horse, he lashed it with his spurs and raced along the narrow path. Terrified by the noise, and seeing an escape to freedom, the horse had no need of a second bidding but fled along the woodland path while the Norman soldier struggled from the fight to follow with all the speed he could. As the Irish were more deeply tangled in the struggle, there were a few precious moments before a few of them detached themselves and set off in pursuit.

Fergus laid his head along the horse's neck and let it race for home. He felt strange and light and his right leg was useless. He stole a moment to look down and all but reeled and fell. Sick with fright at the red blood spreading across the grey flanks of the horse from the yawning wound in his leg, he could do no more than cling blindly and hope that his horse would do the rest. He heard Simon close behind him, urging him to hold his grip, and, farther back, through the buzz of his bewildered head, he heard the hoof-beats of the men who were chasing them. Only the change of light told him when they left the forest, and as he looked up to sec the castle, it swung and tilted in a scarlet mist. But he knew that there was something they must do.

"Your horn, Simon," he croaked; but it was not necessary. Even as he tried to speak, the horn rang out across the fields. It was the last sound the boy remembered.

In the castle, the horn alerted the sentries on the gate. As they looked down from the tower, they saw the two horses thundering across the grass and their pursuers bursting from the woods behind them.

"It is the Irish prince," yelled the sentry who had seen the boy go out.

On an instant order, the drawbridge started down and the long screech of the portcullis was drowned in the blare of horns that sounded the alert. Soldiers ran to the ramparts from their quarters in the Bailey. As they saw the drawbridge drop down, the Irish realized that they had lost their chance. They checked their horses and took their bows to try to pick the boy from off his horse's back before he reached the castle. Their answer was a shower of Norman arrows, under cover of which Fergus and the soldier thundered into shelter. Some instinct told the unconscious boy that he was safe and he loosed his grip on his horse's neck and tumbled to the ground. It was Guilbert at whose feet he fell. The man spat and turned away.

"If I had my way, the drawbridge would have stayed up and left him with his fellow brigands. My lord, your pardon."

He flushed and stepped aside as Sir Jocelin, who had come from the keep on hearing the alert, went swiftly to the boy, who had now been picked up by some men-at-arms.

"He is not dead but very badly wounded," he said. "Take him carefully to his solar and call the surgeon and my Lady Blanche. Now, Guilbert, bring that soldier to the guard-room so that I can learn what has happened."

Sometime later when the surgeon had cleaned and bound Fergus's wound and the Lady Blanche had given him a soothing drink and left him resting, Sir Jocelin came quietly to the room where the boy was lying. A brazier glowed against the damp air, for the boy still shivered under the woollen covers of his bed, despite the great coverlet of white fur that had been thrown across him. One of Lady Blanche's maids was seated at his side.

"Go now, Janine," said Sir Jocelin. "I want to speak alone with the boy."

"My lord," the girl curtsied and slipped out through the door.

The knight eased himself onto the low stool which she had left. It was a few moments before the boy realized there had been any change. When he opened his eyes and saw who was sitting beside him, his white face took on a look of desperate anxiety.

"My lord," he began in a voice that he had to strain even to reach a whisper.

"Do not try to talk too much, Fergus," said the knight. "It is wrong for me to trouble you while your wound is so fresh, but I must ride out from Ardrohan within the next few hours, and what you are able to tell me may mean a great deal in the work that I have to do."

The boy clearly was not listening. He strained to speak again.

"My lord, oh, my lord, I do ask your pardon. Have many of your men been killed? If so, it is my fault because I agreed to treachery, however much I may deceive myself by saying I gave no word. But in the end, I myself proved to be the one who was deceived."

Sir Jocelin looked at the harassed, ashen face. "You must be peaceful, Fergus. I do not know why you blame yourself. From what I know, your escort were attacked in the forest and you kept your promise most honorably and rode full speed for Ardrohan rather than attempt to escape."

"Oh," the boy whispered, "if only it had really been like that! No, my lord, I blame myself in that I knew that something of this kind might happen and I did not tell you."

The knight's long, narrow face grew stern. "I think you had better tell me now," he said.

Slowly and weakly, Fergus told the tale of Brother Colman's message, and Sir Jocelin listened, severe and intent.

"And why did you not tell me?" he said at the end. "Did you not feel that your oath bound you to do so?"

The boy's white face flushed miserably. "My lord," he whispered in a voice so faint that the tall knight had to bend to hear him. "I was afraid that you would stop me going for lessons."

Sir Jocelin straightened up and his stern face softened and broke into a smile. He laid his hand on the boy's, deep in the soft, white fur.

"Indeed," he said, amusement in his voice, "truly a child's reason. We must not expect too much of you; you are still very young."

Fergus's anxious face relaxed a little. "My lord," he asked, "you will not blame Brother Colman? It was not his fault, for he only passed the message."

"He had a duty, as I had trusted him with you and your sister. He could have told the sergeant of the troop. He is not a child. No, Fergus, you must leave the monk to me. But there is one thing I still do not understand. When the ambush did take place as you expected it, why did you not fly with your people? Why did you not go with your father?"

"My father!" The boy struggled to raise himself in the bed, his blue eyes wide upon Sir Jocelin's face. "It was not my father. It was my uncle Felim, who is trying to take my father's throne. It was not rescue, but a plot to kill me. My death was almost my reward for my dishonesty to you."

The knight eased him gently back onto his pillow. His face was thoughtful.

"I see," he said. "You think, then, that your father had no part in this?"

"No, no. My uncle Felim is my father's enemy."

At this moment the door burst open and Grania rushed into the room.

"Fergus," she cried, "I was down in the falcon mews and nobody knew where to find me. Are you . . . my lord," she

101

said, halting and drawing back, "I beg your pardon. I did not notice you."

"Come, see your brother, Grania. T"he knight stood up, his height and presence filling the small shadowy room. "He looks very poorly now, but the surgeon tells us there is nothing that his youth won't heal quickly with rest and care. He has lost a great deal of blood."

"But what happened?" asked Grania, shaken by the boy's white face, the color of the fur robe under which he was lying.

"It was our uncle Felim, Grania," he whispered wearily, "he tried to kill me once again."

"Felim!" cried Grania, and started to say something else. Then her voice trailed away in silence as she looked at the knight. She saw that the small light of the brazier flickered on chain mail and not upon the softer clothes he usually wore when he was inside the castle. She spoke again after a long pause.

"My lord," she said, "I see you are armed. Are you going to fight?"

"I am, my child."

"And whom do you fight?" Grania's throat felt thick.

"Well you know, Grania, but I would not have gone without telling you." His face was soft with pity. He glanced at the bed and saw that Fergus's white lids had closed. "Your brother is asleep. Come with me for a moment, and I will tell you what I must do."

They went into the Lady Blanche's solar, where she sat with her spinning. With one quick look at both their faces, she said nothing but smiled at Grania and bent her head over her work. Sir Jocelin sat down in a chair and motioned Grania to a stool beside him.

"I must go again and seek your father, Grania, and this time I must find him. Within the next few months, King John, himself, will visit Ireland and I must account my reasons for having part of Connacht unsubdued. He is angry that I have not yet either destroyed, or reached agreement with, your father and so I must do this as soon as I can. I most deeply hope that it will be the second course. We know he cannot be too far away for he was in Athenmore last night." The knight began to laugh, shaking his head: "I cannot but admire him, Grania, and I find the same high humor in your little coxcomb brother, Fergus. It is clear that the Red King is followed only by a handful of his tribe who must lie with him somewhere in hiding. He can get no help from his other tribes scattered in different villages for we have them under far too strict a watch. So he knows he has not got the strength to fight and concentrates, instead, on being a nuisance—and most successfully."

"How so, my lord?"

"Last night he came to Athenmore with a small body of men and overcame the guard without a sound, but not before one of them recognized him. Then he drove all the cattle from the pens outside the castle walls away into the forest. But not to steal them, no!" The knight laughed again. "He let them loose within the woods in small groups so that today half the garrison of the keep is in the forest rounding up the cattle! He knows how to make us Normans waste our time."

Grania laughed delightedly. "My father, as you say, is like my brother. They laugh easily and love a jest." Then she thought of the full meaning of the knight's words and, for a long minute, her fingers plucked the soft wool of her dress. "My lord," she said at last, "I beg of you . . . I know you have your duty to your king, but . . ." Tears welled up in her eyes and she could say no more.

Sir Jocelin stood up and, laying his hand for a moment on her head, he went swiftly from the room.

During the afternoon, Fergus awoke to find Grania sitting on the stool beside his bed.

"How are you now, Fergus?" she asked him.

"I am better," said the boy, "my head is clearer and I do not feel so strange. Has the troop returned from the forest?"

"Yes. Our uncle Felim is dead. They knew he was the leader so they brought him in to find out who he was. Sir Jocelin asked me to be brave enough to look at him and see if it was Felim." She gulped hard and pressed her hands up to her eyes. "It was so ugly, and that beast Guilbert laughed at me for being upset."

"I hate Guilbert," said Fergus weakly. "It is a good thing his business keeps him to the Outer Bailey so that we don't often see him." He spoke vaguely as if he found it hard to think of what he said. "So my uncle Felim is dead," he went on. "I am glad. It is one less threat to our good father's life."

Grania thought of the mighty troop of men-at-arms which she had seen assembling in the Outer Bailey when they had taken her to look at Felim's body. "Yes," she said wearily, "one less threat. Now you must sleep again, for you need rest more than anything."

She moved across the solar and leaned against the cold stone of the window. On a clear day she could see the tips of her beloved mountains that lay beyond Duncormac; but today was cloudy.

One less threat! At least Sir Jocelin once again had not thought to ask her if she knew where her father's hideout was. If the Red King was taken on this foray, it would not be for her telling. In the heavy silent day she heard clearly the whine of the descending drawbridge and the hollow drumming of the horses' hooves as Sir Jocelin and his soldiers rode out of the castle.

Fergus's wound healed well, as the surgeon had promised, and by the middle of the summer he was limping round the castle, joining in the games of the other boys for a short while. Grania had never told him what Sir Jocelin had said to her, that this time her father must come to terms or die, for she felt it would hold him back from getting well. So he recovered happily, unaware of the reason for Sir Jocelin's absence, now prolonged into many weeks. But he still tired quickly, and one summer day as Grania sat in the window of her solar, she watched him separate himself from a crowd of tumbling boys and limp slowly towards the Ladies' garden, which lay below her.

Since Sir Jocelin had gone away, she often sat at this window gazing across at the blue mountaintops which she had looked at so often from home. She thought of her father nowadays more than ever, remembering his great voice and his hot temper and his fierce, short ways with his enemies. She had never feared him, for she knew the gentleness and wisdom that lay beneath his thundering ways and she hoped desperately that he and Sir Jocelin would come to speech before either of them drew his sword. If this could only be contrived, she felt all would be well. Sir Jocelin already knew much about her father and thought of him with admiration. If the obstinate and willful king would only pause long enough to get to know the knight, then she felt sure they would find a way to come to terms.

She saw Fergus pause at the entry to the garden and look up at her window. He beckoned her to come down. She picked up her rose-red skirts and ran down the little circular stair, out of the big door and down the wide stone staircase on the outside wall. At the foot of this lay the entry to the Ladies' garden, laid out for the pleasure of the Lady Blanche, who was sitting there at this moment with attendants.

Fergus met Grania as she came through the flowering hedge that edged the garden.

"Come and sit with me for a while," he said. "My leg hurts and I must rest." They walked through the garden to where the Lady Blanche was sitting.

"Oh," cried Grania suddenly, dropping on her knees among the flowers, "look at the little orchids that my lady brought from France, they are in flower!" She picked one, gazing with delight at the fragile purple flower, and took it to Lady Blanche. "See, madam!" she curtsied swiftly, "your little orchids are in bloom. Aren't they beautiful? And yesterday they were only tight closed buds!"

Lady Blanche admired the flower and exclaimed with pleasure that they had grown so successfully. Then she swept aside her spreading skirt and placed Grania on the stone seat beside her, putting into the child's hands the bright silks with which she was working. Fergus stretched himself on the short grass at her feet and there, in the warm sunlight, the children sat and chattered in their fluent Norman French and gazed at the now familiar scene before them.

This was the private, or family, side of the huge castle. The wide stone stairs which led up from the sloping garden to the Great Hall were used only by the ladies and nobles who shared the family life. The servants and the men-at-arms used the other entry on the ground floor in the opposite wall, which led into the Lower Hall, where they lived. Beyond the fragrant hedges round the garden was the great open space which the children had learned to call the Inner Bailey. Here all the entertainments of the castle took place, the cock-fighting and the bear-baiting, the jousting, wrestling and sports. If the weather was unkind all these could be watched in comfort from the windows of the Hall or from the ladies' solars. Here, too, the little boys ran and played and fought and made their endless games of men-at-arms. There were many buildings round the edges of the Bailey and underneath the high walls there were the church, the wooden houses of the upper servants, the stables of Sir Jocelin and the nobles and the mews where Grania loved to go and stroke the soft plumage of the hooded falcons.

Grania's eyes moved over all this and then lifted, as they always did in the end, to the great walls on top of which the sentries marched in ceaseless watchfulness. She always held a hope that one day a sentry would raise a shout and it would prove to be her father riding with Sir Jocelin, as the knight wished, in peace. But if he would not come in peace, what then? Every day she waited for some news, almost frightened of anything that she might hear. Many things in Ardrohan had become so dear to her that she would find it difficult to leave them. The little girl liked the formal manners of the Norman castle, and she had long since lost her heart to the dark-haired Lady Blanche. As for Sir Jocelin, she held him in such wonder that she was almost speechless in his presence. Yet against the knight's dark dignity, she always had in mind the picture of her father, tall and heavy-shouldered with his long red hair and quick impetuous movements. Torn between these two, she had long ago stopped hoping that one would be the victor. Her only happiness lay in the unlikely hope of peace. She fretted in this way as she sat in the warm scented garden and smoothed the bright silks on her lap and watched the colors glowing as they caught the sun. One of the ladies was singing, a little tinkling French song which seemed to have no end and no beginning.

It ended abruptly as the old seneschal of the castle came hurrying round the keep and entered the garden from below. He was a heavy, awkward man but now he hurried in such obvious excitement that he positively skipped along the path, his face lit up with pleasure. The ladies had to turn away in case they should offend him with their smiles.

He bowed as best he could before Lady Blanche. "My lady," he gulped, beaming and gasping so that he could hardly speak, "a messenger has just arrived. Sir Jocelin will be with us in a few hours. He has been lying at Athenmore."

The Lady Blanche stood up. But even as her face lit up with delight, she thought of the child beside her. Grania had not moved.

"And what did the man say, Hugo?" she asked the old servant. "Did Sir Jocelin . . . ?"

Hugo looked kindly at the children, but answered Lady Blanche. "No, my lady, he did not find the Red King. He comes home safe with all his men."

Fergus started from the ground; his face was puzzled and his mouth open on a question. His sister laid a hand upon his arm. "Not now, Fergus. I will tell you presently. It is enough that they are both safe."

The boy was silent and Lady Blanche turned and spoke to Hugo. "We have not much time. Tell the scullions to make haste and give us of their best. Fresh rushes must be brought to lay the Hall and the vintners are to draw the finest wines. We ladies must away and put on all our grandest clothes. Our gentlemen have been away too long. Grania, get another girl to help you and gather scented flowers to strew among the rushes so that we can dine with pleasant perfume."

"I will help," cried Fergus, "for with my leg like this I am little better than a girl." He was anxious for a chance to talk to Grania.

Lady Blanche smiled at him. "Very well. And Grania, braid your hair, my lord would not think it fitting to see that flying gold."

She turned and went up the stairs with her ladies. The old steward scuttled back the way he had come and the children rushed to do as she had asked. In flat rush baskets, they gathered all the scented flowers they could find, talking as they picked until Fergus understood all about Sir Jocelin's absence. They gathered musk and rosemary and marjoram, roses and heavy clove carnations and the small sweet lilies that Lady Blanche loved so much.

"We must have some of the purple orchids," cried Grania, "even if they have no scent." But having picked them, she could not bear to think of them being trampled underfoot. "I know," she said. "I will get a little cup and place them by Lady Blanche's plate so that she can enjoy them while she is eating."

They filled their baskets over and over again, and Grania ran up with them to the Great Hall and scattered them where the servants had cleaned the floor and laid it with rushes they had gathered from the moat. Excited by the prospect of a feast, they poked their noses in the kitchens off the Lower Hall only to be chased out by the short-tempered scullions, struggling as they were in so short a time to dress and cook the swans and peacocks, the herons and wild geese and the French marchpane and sugar cakes.

When everything was ready and the children had been approved in their best clothes, they climbed up the winding stair in the corner tower with Lady Blanche until they stood upon the battlements themselves. Here they were above the curtain walls and the tops of the trees and, oven in the hazy distance, they could see the formidable keep of Athenmore.

"I have heard that King John himself rests there at Athenmore," said Lady Blanche. "My lord will have been with him if that is so."

The children looked at one another and then turned back to watch the spot where the road emerged from the forest. They looked to see the first horseman ride out from the trees, for the forest was so thick they could not see them sooner.

Suddenly Fergus cried out, "Madam, I swear I see points of light among the trees! It is the sunlight on their mail!"

The ladies crowded and argued but Fergus proved to be right and the first riders came from the shelter of the trees on to the open road and across the grass. From this height they looked like toys, but Lady Blanche could just recognize her husband's standard borne before him by his squire. But there was another standard carried in front of the knight's. And who was the horseman riding with him? Lady Blanche strained her eyes against the sun and gasped.

"It is! In truth it is! The royal standard! King John himself has ridden from Athenmore with Sir Jocelin." The ladies chattered and fluttered, but Lady Blanche had regained her calm. "Everything is well. There is nothing unprepared. He shall sleep in the best solar." Her eyes fell on Grania and Fergus who had moved together as if for protection. "What is the matter, children? You have done well. Because of you the king shall dine as in a summer garden and I shall tell him of your efforts."

"My lady," it was Grania who spoke, "I am afraid. The king will not harm us?"

"You have nothing to fear. Sir Jocelin would permit no one to harm you, for you are his wards. And remember, you, too, are a king's daughter so bear yourself as one and do not show my cousin John you fear him. He is very proud himself and admires pride in others."

"I will look after you, Grania," cried Fergus boldly. "I fear no English king!"

"Then, our bantling," Lady Blanche answered him gently, "I would be civil and a little careful, for my cousin's pride is touchy and you would find it easy to offend him with ill manners. Now let us go down and meet them, or our royal guest will reach the Hall before we do and that, in itself, would be the worst of manners."

As they left the battlements, the cavalcade was sweeping round them to the Outer Bailey and the main portcullis. Grania paused to glance once more at the shorter figure riding beside Sir Jocelin and then turned away and followed Fergus down the stairs.

They waited outside the door of the Great Hall. Lady Blanche stood at the top of the steps and placed the children a little to one side. Her ladies were grouped behind her and also those nobles who had remained in the castle in case of an attack in the absence of Sir Jocelin. Grania heard the whine of the drawbridge going down, the screech of the portcullis and the clatter of hooves across the Outer Bailey. The party swept across the inner drawbridge and round the keep and drew rein below the garden. The servants ran to take the horses, and Sir Jocelin led the king up towards the group on the stairs.

"My liege," said Lady Blanche sinking into a deep obeisance, "I bid you welcome to our home."

The king took her hands and raised her up, kissing her warmly. "My dear, dear cousin," he said, "what a long time since we have met. We were only children then."

All the nobles in the order due to their rank were presented to the king, and then Sir Jocelin drew Grania and Fergus towards him. "Sire, these are my two Irish wards of whom I told you. The children of our elusive King of Connacht."

Grania sensed unease in the knight's voice, and as she rose from her deep curtsey, she looked up and met the king's eyes. They held hers only for a second and then he shrugged and turned away; in that second, fear had filled her again. Sir Jocelin was very powerful, but this was England's king and she had read no kindness in his eyes. Thin and restless, he came up only to the knight's shoulder and Grania secretly thought that Sir Jocelin was far more noble. There was in King John's face something which she felt she could not trust.

"He is not half the man our father is!" whispered Fergus in her ear. "I don't like his pinched and miserable face!"

Grania shushed him urgently and laid her hand on his arm as they joined in the procession which moved into the Great Hall. They took their places at the long tables, and very soon the feast began as the serving men rushed in the hot food, still fresh upon the roasting spits. As there was so much company, the children were at a low table and, strain as she might, Grania could not hear a word of the conversation at the top, where Sir Jocelin and his nobles were seated round the unsmiling king. Fergus, being younger, could not be downcast and settled to enjoy the feast as the castle minstrel played and sang and the tumblers and jesters came and went. Grania, however, waited for the long uneasy meal to end; she was uneasy because she sensed the discord between Sir Jocelin and the king and because, again and again, she felt herself and the unheeding Fergus fixed by King John's unfriendly eyes. She felt certain that they themselves were, in some way, the cause of the disagreement.

She forgot her anxiety for a few moments, as Sir Jocelin's jester leaned across the table to make sport with her and beat her about the head with his jingling bells when she could find no answer to his riddles. As she laughed and fended off the soft attack, she felt a touch on her shoulder.

"Little madam," said a servant at her side, "Sir Jocelin bids you to go to the high table. I think King John wishes to speak to you and your brother."

She grasped Fergus, who had seized the jester's bells and was about to turn the riddles back on him, and told him what they were bidden. He looked surprised and puzzled. "What does the mean-faced one want with us?" he said truculently.

"Oh, hush, my foolish brother," said Grania. "Listen, I know you are my father's heir and I am only your sister, but believe me that in what the king is going to speak about, I *do* know more than you. Hold your peace and let me do the talking. It matters a great deal."

With a quick change of mood so like his father, Fergus grew solemn and held his arm out to his sister. "I trust you in all things, Grania. Now let's go and see what we must face."

With the same grave dignity that he had shown at his election, he led her round the tables and they walked up the middle of the Hall.

"Remember you are a king's daughter. Do not show my cousin that you fear him." Lady Blanche's words came into Grania's mind and she lifted up her head. The Hall along which she had so often run and skipped seemed endless as it stretched away before them to the High Table. A silence fell as the children walked up the Hall and the eyes of the company flickered from them to the glowering king. She walked steadily with her hand on Fergus's and her back so straight that it hurt her. Their feet disturbed the rushes as they moved and threw up the perfume of the flowers they had picked so blithely that afternoon. She knew the king was watching them but she kept her eyes fixed on the warm, kind gaze of the knight beside him. She gained confidence as she came up the long room, and when at last she stood below the king and turned her eyes to him, it was with calm and dignity.

She curtsied and Fergus bowed beside her.

"My liege," she said, "you wished to speak with us?"

"Indeed, I wish to speak with you." King John's face was pinched with rage. "But even more I wish to speak with your villain father. He has been allowed his freedom for too long. He is a menace and a persecution to our reign. Tell me, do you know where he is?"

Grania's grip tightened on her brother's arm. Here, in one second, from the king, was the question that Sir Jocelin had not thought of asking in three years. Now she had to give an answer.

Before she could speak, the king lurched to his feet, crashing his fist upon the table. "You know," he shouted. "Your face tells me that you know. Tell me! Tell me, or I swear I will have you killed!"

Grania looked him in the face, her eyes were steady. "Yes, Sire," she said quietly, "I do know where he is."

She saw Sir Jocelin half-rise out of his chair with a startled exclamation and felt rather than saw the amazement on her brother's face. But he kept quiet. As calmly as she could, she went on, "And if you kill me, my liege, then you will never know, for I alone have the secret."

Her quietness served to enrage the king further. "And your brother brat?" he snarled. "Does he also know what your king must not be told?" He glared at Fergus.

114

Grania squeezed his arm to hold him silent. "He knows nothing," she said quickly. "He was too young."

"But you know!"

"Yes," Grania glanced desperately at Sir Jocelin.

"Well, then, tell. TELL!"

"No," she said in a whisper.

"Then upon my soul . . ." The king leaned across the table, his face working. "I will leave no Irishman alive in Connacht, and I will make a start with you and with your speechless brother."

Sir Jocelin rose. "Sire," he said quietly, "I beg you—this is not the way."

The king stared at him vacantly for some seconds as if he did not understand, then slumped suddenly in his chair and hunched a pettish shoulder towards the knight. "Do as you wish," he said, "do as you wish. 'Tis you who rule here in Connacht and not I. And i' faith, I must say," he straightened up, his rage easing, "you have made great peace. With the exception of this devil, Cormac." He glared again at the children.

"Grania," Sir Jocelin's voice was quiet and his eyes reassuring. "Do you truly know where your father is hiding?"

"Yes, my lord. I am sure I do."

"Why then did you never tell me?"

"You never asked, my lord, and I was grateful for this mercy, as the secret was not mine to tell. Not even to my brother." She turned and gave a small, faint smile to Fergus. "In the months before the burning of Duncormac, my father taught me how to get into a very secret place. Fergus would have been told at the same age. I am sure that the Red King is hiding there now. Even if you had asked me I could not tell you because my father swore me to the secret." For a moment

115

her lip trembled. She had found the knowledge a heavy burden when it would have pleased Sir Jocelin to have told him and perhaps helped to turn her father from his willfulness. But she had promised.

"But Grania, you knew that I was seeking your father to make peace and not to destroy him."

There was a violent and impatient movement from the king. The cup beside the Lady Blanche's plate was overturned and the purple flowers were scattered at the children's feet. Gazing down at them, Grania came to her decision.

She looked up at Sir Jocelin. "My lord, I could carry a message to him for you, to tell him this."

They both stared at her and she felt Fergus move restlessly at her side.

"You alone," said Sir Jocelin after a moment. "I would not permit it."

"Fergus could come with me. The Red King would wish to see his son. If you would send me with some men-at-arms to a spot I can show them on the borders of the Yellow Bog, then they must leave me there at dusk and come back and meet me two days later. I will bring my father, or if he refuses to come, then I promise you we will come back alone."

The king snorted. "He would not let you," he said contemptuously.

"My father, Sire, honors his promises and he would honor mine."

A flush crept up the king's face. All England at this day was ringing with the tale of how *he* kept his promises.

"I do not like it, Grania. You are only twelve years old and it is not safe. I' faith, I am proud that you want to do this for me." Sir Jocelin smiled at her, anxiety and affection mixed upon his face.

She smiled back. "For you, my lord, and for my father. We can meet no one but our own people beyond the place where your men will leave me. We may go tomorrow night?"

"So be it. The sooner it is done, the better. We will talk about it in the morning. Now go to the ladies; the king has done with you."

King John waved a disinterested hand and the children bowed. As they left, Grania saw that he still sat with his chin in his hand, his face dark and his brooding eyes fixed on them. There was no doubt that he was not satisfied to let the children go alone.

Grania parried Fergus's excited questions, assuring him that by the next night he would know as much as she did. He went off to join the children in a game but Grania climbed the stairs to the gallery above the Hall, for she wanted to be quiet and to think about what she had promised to do. It would not be easy, especially as Fergus was still slow on his wounded leg.

As she stood in the shadow of the pillars and looked down on the Hall below, she saw something which filled her with apprehension. Guilbert, the Constable of Ardrohan, who had wanted to kill them when they were first discovered and who had been hostile to them ever since, now approached the king and talked to him. Grania knew that he had been sitting close enough to hear the conversation at the High Table and now she watched him expounding some plan, at great length, to the king. She saw a slow, crooked smile creep across the king's face, followed by a nod of gratified assent. She sighed. She knew as clearly as if she had been warned that the expedition to her father would not go exactly as she and Sir Jocelin would plan it.

Chapter XIII

Early the following day the king rode from Ardrohan on his journey back to Athenmore. Grania saw no more of him except to watch him from the window of her solar as he rode with his train across the Bailey. When she heard the drawbridge whining down behind the last of the procession, she ran to look for Sir Jocelin.

"My lord, if we are going today, we must not be too late. It is many hours on horseback to the Yellow Bog."

Guilbert was beside the knight's chair, giving his day's report on his men-at-arms. He looked at Grania smoothly, his coarse face creased into a mask of pleasant helpfulness. "Indeed, yes," he said silkily. "It is a long journey, my little lady, and you do not want to hurry in case you are too tired for the part of your travels that may be left."

Sir Jocelin moved restlessly. "Grania, I don't like this at all, but it seems to me to be our only hope, for I respect your promise to your father and would not force your secret from you. But the king grows restive and will soon lose his patience and invade Connacht, and this would mean that all our work for peace was for no purpose. It would, in fact, end my hopes of seeing your father once again upon his throne. But won't you

take some of my men with you all the way and swear them to
secrecy?"

"Sir, I cannot. My father asked me to tell no one. He said
that once too many know a secret, it *is* no longer a secret.
No, my lord, we will be with your men until we reach the
Yellow Bog and after that . . ." She lifted her eyes and looked
Guilbert full in the face. He dropped his own and shuffled the
rushes at his feet. "After that," she went on, "we must just
look after ourselves."

Sir Jocelin agreed reluctantly to her plan and then told her
to wait for a moment. He went over to the golden casket and
took out the Holy Book. "Give this to your father as a token
of my sincerity."

"My lord, I thank you. This will mean a great deal and it
will say more than I can tell him."

So, late in the morning, Grania and Fergus rode out once
more from Ardrohan with their troop of men-at-arms. The
knight and Lady Blanche had bidden them the fondest of
good-byes and as they rode along the open road, the children
looked up and waved to the tiny figures that watched them
from the battlements. But even as she waved and laughed at
Fergus flapping with his russet cloak, Grania watched carefully to see if they were followed. By the time they had entered the forest, however, she had seen no one else leave the
castle and was free for the moment to enjoy her journey. She
could not help but be excited at the thought of going back to
see her father, however difficult the way, and, after the unaccustomed summer months inside the castle, she was delighted
to be riding in the sunlit woods again. The track they rode
along was wide and beaten hard but edged with moss and
flowers and spattered with a shifting gold as the sunshine
filtered through the tall branches that arched over their heads.

In order not to tire his leg by having to hold his own horse, Fergus rode in front of a soldier and they sang a gay French round together. As the deep bass chimed against the boy's light voice, Grania looked at her brother and suddenly saw him with her father's eyes—a little Norman with his fair hair cropped and speaking French more easily than Irish. Her heart sank. Had she changed as much? The Red King would not be pleased, and that would make her task for peace more difficult. But just as she looked at him, Fergus caught her eye and laughed, his great uproarious laugh for laughing's sake, and Grania saw him so much like her father, for all his Norman ways, that she laughed back and pushed away her doubts. All would be well, if she could get him safely to the Red King.

They journeyed through the long summer afternoon and stopped for only one short rest to eat the loaves and cheese that they had brought and to let the horses drink from a small stream. They came out of the woods and crossed the open fields that lay between them and the Yellow Bog just as the sun slipped behind the westward hills. Grania peered round the leading soldiers at what lay ahead and her courage almost failed her. As far as the eye could see lay the desolation of the bog, colorless and dead in the cold light of the approaching dusk. The only sound came from the plaintive curlews and the only movement from the ghostly drifts of white bog cotton as it swayed in the cool evening wind. She gathered herself together. This was not the moment to let herself be frightened. She looked carefully at the distant hills and the position of the setting sun and instructed Michael to alter his direction. They soon came to a rough road set above the bog at the edge of the firm meadows and once again Grania looked at the hills. Then she watched carefully at the side of the road and by some sign which only she could see, she called the cavalcade to a halt.

"Here you must leave us, Michael. Will you be able to find the place in two days' time?"

"Well, my little madam," the kindly soldier shook his head, "I don't like leaving you at all but 'tis Sir Jocelin's orders that we should do everything you say." He looked east and west along the bog. "This road is so straight that we should see you from anywhere. God bless you now and the young prince also and send you good work." He wheeled his horse and led his soldiers at a gallop back across the flat land towards the forest.

Grania took one long searching look along the edge of the trees and then turned and faced the bog. "Now, Fergus, I must repeat the words I said to you last evening. I am only your sister and you are my father's heir but if you wish us both to survive you must obey my every, smallest order."

Fergus's fair face glimmered in the dusk beside her. "And I give you the same answer, sister. I trust you in all things. But believe me, I do not like the look of this bog!"

"I don't either, Fergus, but I know my way. My father told me to find the place to start like this. When the Mountain of the Witch and the Mountain of the Stones moved together into one against the setting sun, then I looked for this." She showed him a stone pillar sunk into the ground beside the road, only the top showing above the sedgy grass. "At the beginning it is quite easy but you must hold on to me closely and walk carefully for if you only fall into a pool, it will be quite hard for me to pull you out." She looked back over her shoulder. "Now we must make haste and get ahead."

"Ahead of whom?"

"You will see," she said, and took his hand.

It was, as she said, quite easy to begin with. The ground was rough and the grass was long and marshy, but it was not too hard even on the boy's lame leg. Only occasionally did

Grania have to guide him round a little reed-grown pool or a patch of treacherous, soft, green grass. It was still light enough for them to see where they were going, even though the sun had now set and only the cold, green light of Irish evening spread across the bog. They were so intent on looking where they stepped that they had no time to think about the lonely waste they crossed.

Only Grania looked up regularly and frequently at the line of hills now lying on their left. "We must keep moving, Fergus," she said when the boy asked for a rest. "We must have got a certain distance before it gets too dark for me to see the hills or I shall not know where we are. It is not far now. Look, this will help us both." She took some bread and cheese which was left over from an earlier meal, from the bag on her back and they ate it as they walked. In this bag she also carried the Holy Book. "This is just about the spot we need to reach," she said presently. "Now we can rest a moment. Fergus! Did you hear anything?"

"I thought I heard horses."

"So did I. So he is here." She turned and peered back across the gathering dark towards the distant road. As it stood so high above the level of the bog, she could see the moving shapes of men and horses clearly against the dimming sky.

"They are dismounting, Grania," Fergus cried. "Who is it?"

"Guilbert," said Grania briefly. "We must light our lanthorns."

"But they will see us, Grania. I dislike that devil Guilbert, and I would put nothing past him."

"He does not seek us, Fergus. He wants to follow us so that he can kill our father. Here, hold the lanthorns, while I light them and we will lead him where he thinks he wants to go."

Fergus saw what lay in Grania's mind and a giggle of
pure mischief burst from him as he held the lanthorn up for
Grania's kindled flame.

"Hold it up, now, so they can see it clearly." Grania smiled,
too, as she saw the dark shapes on the road slip down into the
shadow of the bog. "It is nice and easy there, it will give them
confidence." She smiled again as she saw lights kindle into
life and start to move across the bog. Then she turned to Fergus
and faced the reality of what they must do. "Now, Fergus, listen carefully. What we have got to do is difficult and dangerous. Look, I will take my girdle and tie it once round my waist
and then round my wrist so if you slip I have three hands to
hold you. We must keep our lanthorns or Guilbert will have
no light to follow. But Fergus, listen: we are in the bog now,
the deadly treacherous bog and we have no path. When our
father showed me this secret way, he bound my eyes and
made me learn it without looking. For he said the day might
come when my feet would need to remember when perhaps
my eyes could not. Now we shall see how well my feet have
learned their lesson. Put your arm round my waist and I will
put mine round yours like this. Now, in the name of God's
grace, each time I bid you . . . *jump!*"

She looked at the evening star hanging in the grape-blue
sky above the hills and faced away from it. She breathed a
prayer and closed her eyes. She called to Fergus and they
jumped, landing awkwardly on a firm tussock, the sheen of
water at their feet. Again and again and again they jumped
through the rapidly darkening evening and their tiny shaken
lights flickered on the water and on the green treacherous
slime that lay between their footholds. Every so often, Grania
paused and they held their lights aloft towards the other tiny
flames which bobbed behind them in the darkness.

Grania was well aware that every jump was pain to Fergus as he landed. Several times he stumbled on the edge of the firm ground and Grania hauled him from the ooze with fear striking at her heart as she heard the sickening squelch of the bog under his feet. Once they both fell and had to scramble wildly for a foothold as the icy water of a bog pool dragged at their already sodden clothes. They lay gasping on the ground.

"Grania, I have lost my light and my leg, my leg! It will not take me farther." Fergus bent moaning over his wound, and fear sharpened Grania's temper.

"A pest on wounded legs," she cried. "They do beset me always. But when my father took me to the Abbey to get you, he said that he would have to take his leg as the leg would not take him, and somehow they managed each other. Let it be the same with you. I cannot stay here and I certainly can't go on without you. As for the light, one is enough for the little way that remains. Come on, Fergus, you are the King's son. You cannot say you failed." She hauled him to his feet. "That's better. There is a path soon and you will find it easier. Come, you are a brave boy."

She held her lanthorn up steadily for a moment and then looked at the star above the hills. "Come, brother." They started off again, but now Grania was listening as she moved and soon the sounds that she expected burst across the silent bog.

First there was a shout, and then another, and another, and soon there was such a bedlam of yells and screeches that the birds rose from the bog in wheeling flocks to add their crying to the din. The children stopped and Grania began to laugh.

"I don't think we shall be followed any farther. Nor do we need to show a light." She quenched her lanthorn as she spoke. "We shall see clearer by the stars when we have reached the path."

Fergus was staring back into the darkness where now no lights shone. "They are in the bog." He began to giggle.

"Yes," said Grania. "Guilbert first, I hope."

"Do you think they will be drowned?"

"There shouldn't be much danger unless they have been so foolish as to step in all at once. They can pull each other out. But they will be very wet and very cross and they will not dare to start for home till dawn." The noise across the darkness had died down and Grania giggled again. "Oh, *very* wet and *very* cross!" They held on to each other for a few minutes, laughing helplessly and then turned back to their journey.

After a while, they reached a little path that was nothing more than a ridge above the bog and for a long time they crept along this fragile foothold. Grania felt her way into the darkness and Fergus clung to her shawl behind. Sometimes even this path failed and they had to jump again over the dark water. They had laughed at Guilbert and his friends but they were cold and wet and very tired by now;

Grania was afraid that if Fergus slipped she would not have the strength to pull him out. The boy had not complained again about his leg but crept along behind her and Grania did not dare to ask him how he was in case he should weaken.

It was so long since Grania had lifted up her head that only her feet told her when they reached the meadow. They both went plodding on with the same painstaking care for some yards before they noticed that the ground was firm.

Then, "Fergus," whispered Grania through her chattering teeth, "it is the meadow. We are here!"

Fergus could not speak. The big tent stood on the highest part of the field, and light was shining through the joins of the skins which made it. In front of it burnt the tall King's Candle, serene and steady in the quiet night. Grania knew she would have seen it long before had she lifted up her eyes to look. She unclasped Fergus's cold hand from the edges of her shawl and took it into hers, walking slowly and numbly towards the lighted tent.

Suddenly her numbness left her and she began to run, never noticing when Fergus fell behind her. She could not find the entry to the tent and stumbled frantically butting at the skins until she burst through into the firelight and the ring of startled men. For one moment she stood quite still, smiling at her father; then she fell into a heap upon the floor.

When she awoke, she was lying wrapped in warm skins beside the blazing fire and, as she moved, a woman put a cup of hot, spiced wine to her lips. With a cry of delight, she recognized Eithne, who kissed her warmly and bade her drink. Grania felt the glow of warmth from the fire and the wine go stealing through her limbs as Eithne stepped back to make way for her father.

He sat down beside her in the rushes and for a long while he looked at her and did not speak. "You came alone across the Yellow Bog," he said at last slowly, "and brought my son as well."

She sat up and leaned against his knees. "Oh, yes. Do you remember how you told me that my feet would remember better than my eyes? They did; it was my brother's feet that troubled me. They did not know the way and one of them was lame. Is he all right? He was very brave and suffered a lot."

"We have him safely. We searched to see if you had come alone and found he had fallen in the field. He is asleep now. But tell me, Grania, why did you come on such a terrible journey? Have the Normans driven you away?" His voice rose. "Have they ill-treated you? My spies told me you were well and happy. It seemed a better life for you than this." He waved his hand round the smoky tent. "So I left well alone. Though by the prophecies of Malachy, it seems I have a Norman son." His tone was angry but Grania saw that his face was soft as he looked across the fire towards the sleeping boy.

"Father!" She grasped him by the arm and looked up into his face. Her mind was misty with exhaustion and the fumes of unaccustomed wine and she could not sort out her thoughts. It all came pouring out, one great confusion of the lovely Lady Blanche, the wicked Guilbert and the good, kind Norman knight who was so chivalrous and noble and so eager for peace; the threats of the irritable king and the return of the Holy Book and the dreadful journey through the bog. The Red King listened to it all without a word except when she told him of what she had done to Guilbert and his men. Then he threw back his red head and roared with laughter.

"By the saints, daughter, I could not have done better were I there myself. And what matter if they were drowned! They are well disposed of." And he laughed again. Then his face sobered. "Grania, you have proved yourself indeed my daughter. Never has a father known my pride. And your brother too, lame as he was, it took great courage for him to play his part and not to hinder you. It moves me to think that you faced such danger for this Norman knight. Now sleep, child, and I will think about all the things that you have told me."

The next day, Cormac walked with his children in the meadow, part of this strange island of firm ground in the heart of the bog. As well as the large tent that served the purpose of a Hall, there were other smaller ones dotted here and there and among them a few women moved and children played their games. Beyond the meadow was a small area of cultivation and a goat or two cropped at the reedy grass. Here were all the people who had escaped from the blackened village on the hill; they eked out a difficult existence and were supplied only with whatever they could bring, with peril, through the bog.

The King stood and watched them in silence for several minutes and then turned to Grania beside him. "It has been on my mind for a long time that my pride and obstinacy have cost these people far too dear. But for me, they could rebuild Duncormac and pursue their works of peace. They could beat their gold and weave their cloth and rear their children, who, in their turn, could learn the arts of beauty from the good monks at Athenmore. And the rest of our tribe throughout Connacht would be free from persecution. I have held them from far too much and it has taken you to make me realize it. Fergus tells me that he has been promised that we reign undisturbed as Kings of Connacht. In fact, we rule with, not under, your Norman friend. It seems to me that he is one a man may treat with, and not lose his honor. I will return with you."

Grania rubbed her face into his sleeve to hide her tears. She was still very tired. "Father," she said as she lifted her head, "I have been thinking a lot about Mairi. Uncle Felim is dead now, and she has no mother. Do you not think we should forgive her, and have her back to live with us?"

"Your kindness does you credit. Yes—she is Felim's child, and we must care for her. But first we must re-start the village, and see to our own people. Then we shall send for her." Then her father laughed. "But you see what will occur if we make peace," he said. He grabbed Fergus by the back of his neck and shook him like a puppy. "We will breed more like this: a Norman Irishman, French speaking! A strange addition to the Morann tribe. Upon my soul, it is an odd creature."

Fergus wriggled free and his father put his arm round his shoulders.

"But, Father," Grania protested, "he does not really look like a Norman. He is much too fair. The Normans are all very dark."

"Ah, yes. Still, I am sure that stranger things than fair-haired Frenchmen will occur if the red-heads and the black can learn to walk in peace together."

The following day, they journeyed back across the bog, this time in comfort on the backs of two tall warriors to whom every one of the children's jumps was but an easy stride. Their father walked in front of them; he was wearing all that had been saved of his ceremonial clothes and complained that he was only a poor and shabby king for such a visit. But Grania was happy to see he did his grumbling with a smile and seemed delighted to be leaving his seclusion.

The children waved and shouted to see Michael already waiting for them as they came towards the road, with a richly harnessed horse for their father. He hardly spoke on the journey to the castle, except when they came out of the forest and faced the great pile of Ardrohan keep, and he looked at its unweathered stone rising ghostly white in the dusk. "By the grave of Brian, daughter, I show great faith in you that I am ready to bury myself within this heap of stones," he said ruefully.

Fergus laughed aloud and her father with him, and Grania was happy to hear them merry again. As they clattered round the keep and she saw Sir Jocelin waiting on the stairs to welcome her father, she knew that she must now take her place behind her brother. Fergus walked up the steps beside the Red King to where Sir Jocelin stood. He bowed.

"My lord," he said, "it is my pleasure to present to you my royal father, Cormac, King of Connacht."

"Sir," the knight answered, "I bid you welcome to my home."

Side by side, the knight and the Red King passed through the great doors of the castle. As they walked beneath the flaring torch on the wall, Fergus turned and smiled at Grania, who came behind him. She knew what lay in his mind. Since the two men walked in peace, their heads were bare and the torchlight shone upon the red head and the black as they passed side by side together through the door.

Fergus gave his hand to Grania and they followed their father and their friend into the Great Hall to the feast which lay prepared.

About the Author

Madeleine Polland spent many childhood holidays in the Irish village of Athenry, often playing in the ruins of King John's castle, "the keep at Athenmore" in this book. Here, in the thirteenth century, the Red King of Connacht surrendered to King John. The descendants of the King of Connacht still live in County Galway, where Mrs. Polland was born; before her marriage she bore the King's family name.

Written in 1961, *Children of the Red King* was the author's first book for children.

CPSIA information can be obtained at www.ICGtesting.com
Printed in the USA
LVOW13s1434240814

400614LV00001BA/136/P